SOLITARY REFINEMENT

JAMES A. LANDRY

Solitary Refinement

This book is written to provide information and motivation to readers. Its purpose is not to render any type of psychological, legal, or professional advice of any kind. The content is the sole opinion and expression of the author, and not necessarily that of the publisher.

Printed in the United States of America.

ISBN   978-1-951913-03-8   (Paperback)
ISBN   978-1-951913-04-5   (Digital)

Lettra Press books may be ordered through booksellers or by contacting:

Lettra Press LLC
30 N Gould St. Suite 4753
Sheridan, WY 82801, USA
1 303-586-1431 | info@lettrapress.com
www.lettrapress.com

ENDORSEMENTS

"J. A. Landry has a writing style that puts you right into the scene and gets right under the skin of his characters."

"When I bought the book, I began reading it right away. Simply stated, I could not put it down, and I finished it within two days. J. A. Landry spins a dynamite adult fiction tale; his writing style puts the reader right into the story, and the characterizations and dialogue are just right."

"As I read, my emotions ran a surprisingly broad gamut in response to the lives and actions that Landry spun together; it is a ride that is at once believable, frightening in its implications, and entertaining. This is a book I will read a second time."

"It [Fool Star] is a ride worth hanging on for as Landry twirls his readers through the psychotic tour of a bohemian rock and roll star."

"I couldn't put this book down! All my questions were answered! The ending in particular was excellent. When the ride is over you are left wanting more! I can't wait to read another J. A. Landry book!"

Dedicated to My Dad,

Norman R. Landry

May he rest in paradise.

ACKNOWLEDGMENTS

Special Thanks

Richard Robinson—Contributor

ACKNOWLEDGMENTS

Special Thanks

Richard Robinson—Contributor

PREFACE

Hydraulic fracturing is a well-stimulation technique in which rock is fractured by a pressurized liquid. The process involves the high-pressure injection of fracking fluid (primarily water, containing sand and other proppants suspended with the aid of gelling agents) into a wellbore to create cracks in the deep-rock formations through which natural gas, petroleum, and brine will flow more freely. When the hydraulic pressure is removed from the well, small grains of hydraulic fracturing proppants (either sand or aluminum oxide) hold the fractures open.

Hydraulic fracturing began as an experiment in 1947, and the first commercially successful application followed in 1950. As of 2016, over 2.5 million frac jobs have been performed worldwide on oil and gas wells; over one million of those are within the United States. Such treatment is generally necessary to achieve adequate flow rates in shale gas, tight gas, tight oil, and coal seam gas wells. Some hydraulic fractures can form naturally in certain veins or dikes.

Hydraulic fracturing is highly controversial in many countries. Its proponents advocate the economic benefits of more extensively accessible hydrocarbons. However, opponents argue that these are outweighed by the environmental impacts, which include the risks of contaminating ground and surface water, causing air and noise pollution and potentially triggering earthquakes, along with the consequential hazards to public health and the environment.

Mechanics

Fracturing in rocks at great depth frequently becomes suppressed by pressure due to the weight of the overlying rock strata and the cementation of the formation. This suppression process is particularly significant in tensile fractures, which require the walls of the fracture to move against this pressure. Fracturing occurs when effective stress is overcome by the pressure of fluids within the rock. The minimum principal stress becomes tensile and exceeds the tensile strength of the material. Fractures formed in this way are generally oriented in a plane perpendicular to the minimum principal stress, and for this reason, hydraulic fractures in well bores can be used to determine the orientation of stresses. In natural examples, such as dikes or vein-filled fractures, the orientations can be used to infer past states of stress.

Veins

Most mineral vein systems are a result of repeated natural fracturing during periods of relatively high-pore fluid pressure. The impact of high-pore fluid pressure on the formation process of mineral vein systems is particularly evident in cracked-seal veins, where the vein material is part of a series of discrete fracturing events, and extra vein material is deposited on each occasion. One example of long-term repeated natural fracturing is in the effects of seismic activity. Stress levels rise and fall episodically, and earthquakes can cause large volumes of connate water to be expelled from fluid-filled fractures. This process is referred to as seismic pumping.

Dikes

Minor intrusions in the upper part of the crust, such as dikes, propagate in the form of fluid-filled cracks. In such cases, the fluid is magma. In sedimentary rocks with a significant water content, fluid at fracture tip will be steam.

History

Fracturing as a method to stimulate shallow hard-rock oil wells dates back to the 1860s. Dynamite or nitroglycerin detonations were used to increase oil and natural gas production from petroleum-bearing formations. On April 25, 1865, Civil War veteran Colonel Edward A. L. Roberts received a patent for an "exploding torpedo." It was employed in Pennsylvania, New York, Kentucky, and West Virginia using liquid and also, later, solidified nitroglycerin. Later still, the same method was applied to water and gas wells. Stimulation of wells with acid, instead of explosive fluids, was introduced in the 1930s. Due to acid etching, fractures would not close completely, resulting in further productivity increase.

Oil and Gas Wells

The relationship between well performance and treatment pressures was studied by Floyd Farris of Stanolind Oil and Gas Corporation. This study was the basis of the first hydraulic fracturing experiment, conducted in 1947 at the Hugoton gas field in Grant County of southwestern Kansas by Stanolind. For the well treatment, one thousand US gallons of gelled gasoline (essentially napalm) and sand from the Arkansas River was injected into the gas-producing limestone formation at 2,400 feet.

The experiment was not very successful as deliverability of the well did not change appreciably. The process was further described by J. B. Clark of Stanolind in his paper published in 1948. A patent on this process was issued in 1949, and exclusive license was granted to the Halliburton Oil Well Cementing Company. On March 17, 1949, Halliburton performed the first two commercial hydraulic fracturing treatments in Stephens County, Oklahoma, and Archer County, Texas. Since then, hydraulic fracturing has been used to stimulate approximately one million oil and gas wells in various geologic regimes with good success.

In contrast, with large-scale hydraulic fracturing used in low-permeability formations, small hydraulic fracturing treatments are commonly used in high-permeability formations to remedy "skin damage," a low-permeability zone that sometimes forms at the rock-borehole interface. In such cases, the fracturing may extend only a few feet from the borehole.

In the Soviet Union, the first hydraulic proppant fracturing was carried out in 1952. Other countries in Europe and Northern Africa subsequently employed hydraulic fracturing techniques including Norway, Poland, Czechoslovakia, Yugoslavia, Hungary, Austria, France, Italy, Bulgaria, Romania, Turkey, Tunisia, and Algeria.

Massive Fracturing

Massive hydraulic fracturing (also known as high-volume hydraulic fracturing) is a technique first applied by Pan American Petroleum in Stephens County, Oklahoma, USA, in 1968. The definition of massive hydraulic fracturing varies somewhat but is generally referenced to treatments injecting greater than about 150 short tons, or approximately 300,000 pounds (136 metric tons), of proppant.

American geologists became increasingly aware that there were huge volumes of gas-saturated sandstones with permeability too low to recover the gas economically. Starting in 1973, massive hydraulic fracturing was used in thousands of gas wells in the San Juan Basin, Denver Basin, the Piceance Basin, and the Green River Basin, and in other hard-rock formations of the western United States. Other tight sandstone wells in the United States made economically viable by massive hydraulic fracturing were in the Clinton-Medina Sandstone and Cotton Valley Sandstone.

Massive hydraulic fracturing quickly spread

in the late 1970s to western Canada; Rotliegend and Carboniferous gas-bearing sandstones in Germany, Netherlands (onshore and offshore gas fields), and the United Kingdom in the North Sea.

Horizontal oil or gas wells were unusual until the late 1980s. Then operators in Texas began completing thousands of oil wells by drilling horizontally in the Austin Chalk and giving massive slick-water, hydraulic-fracturing treatments to the wellbores. Horizontal wells proved much more effective than vertical wells in producing oil from tight chalk; sedimentary beds are usually nearly horizontal, so horizontal wells have much larger contact areas with the target formation.

Shales

Due to shale's low permeability, technological

research, development, and demonstration were necessary before hydraulic fracturing was accepted for commercial application to shale gas deposits. In 1976, the United States government started the Eastern Gas Shales Project, a set of dozens of public-private hydraulic fracturing demonstration projects. During the same period, the Gas Research Institute, a gas industry research consortium, received approval for research and funding from the Federal Energy Regulatory Commission.

In 1997, taking the slick-water fracturing technique used in East Texas by Union Pacific Resources (now part of Anadarko Petroleum Corporation), Mitchell Energy (now part of Devon Energy), applied the technique in the Barnett Shale of North Texas. This made gas extraction widely economical in the Barnett Shale and was later applied to other shales. George P. Mitchell has been called the "father of fracking" because of his role in applying it in shales. The first horizontal well in the Barnett Shale was drilled in 1991, but was not widely done in the Barnett until it was demonstrated that gas could be economically extracted from vertical wells in the Barnett.

As of 2013, massive hydraulic fracturing is being applied on a commercial scale to shales in the United States, Canada, and China. Several additional countries are planning to use hydraulic fracturing.

Process

According to the United States Environmental Protection Agency (EPA) hydraulic fracturing is a process to stimulate a natural gas, oil, or geothermal energy well to maximize extraction. EPA defines the broader process as including the acquisition of source water, well construction, well stimulation, and waste disposal.

Method

A hydraulic fracture is formed by pumping fracturing fluid into a wellbore at a rate sufficient to increase pressure at the target depth (determined by the location of the well casing perforations) to exceed that of the fracture gradient (pressure gradient) of the rock. The fracture gradient is defined as pressure increase per unit of depth relative to density and is usually measured in pounds per square inch, per square foot, or bars. The rock cracks, and the fracture fluid permeates the rock, extending the crack further and further, and so on.

Fractures are localized as pressure drops off with the rate of frictional loss, which is relevant to the distance from the well.

Operators typically try to maintain fracture width or slow its decline following treatment by introducing a proppant into the injected fluid–a material such as grains of sand, ceramic, or other particulate–thus preventing the fractures from closing when injection is stopped and pressure is removed. Consideration of proppant strength and prevention of proppant failure becomes more important at greater depths where pressure and stresses on fractures are higher. The propped fracture is permeable enough to allow the flow of gas, oil, salt water, and hydraulic fracturing fluids to the well.

During the process, fracturing fluid leak-off (loss of fracturing fluid from the fracture channel into the surrounding permeable rock) occurs. If not controlled, it can exceed 70 percent of the injected volume. This may result in formation matrix damage, adverse formation fluid interaction, and altered fracture geometry, thereby decreasing efficiency.

The location of one or more fractures along the length of the borehole is strictly controlled by various methods that create or seal holes in the side of the wellbore. Hydraulic fracturing is performed in cased wellbores, and the zones to be fractured are accessed by perforating the casing at those locations.

Hydraulic-fracturing equipment used in oil and natural gas fields usually consists of a slurry blender, one or more high-pressure, high-volume fracturing pumps (typically, powerful triplex or quintuplex pumps) and a monitoring unit. Associated equipment includes fracturing tanks, one or more units for storage and handling of proppant, high-pressure treating iron, a chemical additive unit (used to accurately monitor chemical addition), low-pressure flexible hoses, and many gauges and meters for flow rate, fluid density, and treating pressure.

Well Types

A distinction can be made between conventional, low-volume hydraulic fracturing, used to stimulate high-permeability reservoirs for a single well, and unconventional, high-volume hydraulic fracturing, used in the completion of tight gas and shale gas wells. High-volume hydraulic fracturing usually requires higher pressures than low-volume fracturing; the higher pressures are needed to push out larger volumes of fluid and proppant that extend farther from the borehole.

Horizontal drilling involves wellbores with a terminal drill-hole completed as a lateral that extends parallel with the rock layer containing the substance to be extracted.

For example, laterals extend 1,500 to 5,000 feet in the Barnett Shale basin in Texas and up to 10,000 feet in the Bakken formation in North Dakota. In contrast, a vertical well only accesses the thickness of the rock layer, typically fifty to three hundred feet. Horizontal drilling reduces surface disruptions as fewer wells are required to access the same volume of rock.

Drilling often plugs up the pore spaces at the wellbore wall, reducing permeability at and near the wellbore. This reduces flow into the borehole from the surrounding rock formation and partially seals off the borehole from the surrounding rock. Low-volume hydraulic fracturing can be used to restore permeability.

I
MACKENZIE KING

The mantra jumps around in mind as he rolls from side to side. Eyes forced shut, the internal chant helps bring quiet to a noisy head. Sleep may come in an hour or two, but sleep will never come without the echoes of the repetitive hymn. Its roots in Dialectical Based Therapy, the simple act is one tool to help ward off early warning signs and crises triggers. He sometimes also pictures a Stop sign coming at him incrementally growing with each affricate.

stop...Stop...STOP

Mack reluctantly opens his eyes, big and

round, wide, like Al Jolson in black face, or a startled Billie "Buckwheat" Thomas. Gathering poise over the wee-morning frustration and clenched teeth, it is a familiar natural progression. He desperately relents and employs a more involved exercise of mindful acceptance. He uses the "What Skills" within mindfulness—observe, describe, and participate—along with the "How Skills"—nonjudgmentally, one-mindfully, and effectively.

My heels weigh atop of the sheeted mattress. The top sheet lay over my toes. My calves rest on the bottom sheet…the top sheet touches the calves at the top. My thighs touch the bottom sheet, and the top sheet falls over the top of them. My backside sits upon the sheet-covered mattress while the top sheet drapes over my midsection and torso. My upper arms and elbows sit on the bottom sheet; my forearms lean on my ribs. My left hand lay on my chest and across my right. My *head relaxes on a pillow.*He breathes deep, forming the script in mind, fallen under the self-induced spell. Accepting the silent suggestions, he escapes in relief from the pressing thought of the words. Automated repetition of breaths taken deeply in, and exhaled slowly through his parted lips, bring forth—bring rise to—peace. A sixth recital delivers sleep.

A dense sourness fills his stomach and agonizingly holds Mack all balled down in a fetal position. He tastes it, and his tongue feels its thick intermixture as he smacks unsticking it from the roof of his mouth. He is awake yet paralyzed in his queen-size bed, a cannonball weighing heavy in his gut. It is no more comforting for his stomach to lie there, but it stalls him from movement, which is entirely more discomforting. Cognizant that he must force-face another day benumbs the morning. The urge to urinate is intense, so he gets up and walks fast, thighs pressed together, and just barely makes it to the master bath. Sitting there relieved, the enslavement nudges further: the forthcoming infusion of elixir invariably cranks him into motion. He rises in a Pavlovian moment.

The carpeted stairs cushion his feet as he treads up toward the kitchen. Textured Greek artisan tiles feel soft. He looks down. The neutral beige color soothes him to the sight; he wiggles his toes. Mack sleepily programs the coffeemaker then swaggers slowly back downstairs as four strong cups distill.

A perpetual lackadaisical mood arrests any automated robotic system that would otherwise fire him up. But there is no system— not anymore. The flame blew out long ago. His stinking itchy body and greasy flaking scalp prompt Mack to shower. Outside of the functional pairing with showers, he shaves when prickling rash or signs of psoriasis threaten. A single-blade razor scrapes around a full salt-and-pepper goatee.

Albeit slow in coming, constant self-scrutiny and ever-occurring improvement necessarily rallies. Yesterday's clothes are good for another day; they're not odiferous or stained. He cannot be bothered choosing garments every morning within a life of no consequence. Who cares? Morning ritual is a tedious and unwelcome chore. A memorably familiar spark of good nature comes all too infrequently, and conjuring the flare is more intense than raising a magic spell.

Uncleanliness, disarray, and clutter sometimes trigger relative action, but motivation comes coupled with spirit. It's not enough that the house may be dusty, floors dirty, or the counters marked and stained. His laundry is piled high, but to

Mack's credit, the small mountain rises from the top of his washer-dryer.

I'll move with the spirit.

Action comes unplanned, impulsively, as he impetuously jumps up from the moment, as though being jolted by the sharp sting of a chair-bee. Existence is entirely thoughtless: acts unravel blindly and spontaneously, any guide coming from dim intuition and darker conscience. He bounds into queued quests to meet the domestic runaround. Completion of even the lightest task delivers a sense of relief and accomplishment. Sadly, Mack cannot plan and perform banking on this knowledge.

Average days come and go cloaked with indifference, slowly, dismally, and uneventfully. They slowly turn into the next like the lethargic, gradual movement of a slimy gastropod. He's got time. All he's got is time: time unmanaged. Mack keeps no time, has no interest in time, and no need for it. There is not a single compelling reason to bend to it or to any schedule. There is but just one thing to schedule—just the one—ever. Time of days does not matter.

He peers inside the crowded medicine cabinet and impatiently skates thirteen light-brown vials onto the bathroom counter then into the bathroom waste can. The sworn-off medications are gone for good, but the hazy, dreamlike by-product state continues to dull the beveled edge of his mind. Doctors who dartboard-diagnosed unbalanced symptoms and prescribed the meds wonder what happened to the troubled man. All things medicinal, along with pesky random thoughts wished away, Mack stows far to the rear of his consciousness. Forefront thoughts, few as may be, altruistically serve him well enough to carry him through the days. Essential hope fosters empty contentment as days and nights seem only to hint betterment month by month.

Faint inner warmth buoys Mack's temperament and calms his mood. Unbridled universal love saturates him, yet no companion love comes. No, it is a lifelong belief that unparameterized, all-encompassing love and goodness constitute the collective world mass, if not even God. But it's his belief. The atomic value of all things, all beings is love. No new eyes join his to seek the coming dawn, but he sits with the blanketed knowledge that warmly wraps his mind: sublime and subtle relief. Weighty, virtuous hope, and the notion that things can always be worse, present themselves. But on account of the weight, those uplifting, in-thought catalysts come stubbed; so, therefore, hardly matter.

Uncomfortable gray-shaded burden drapes over Mack's shoulders and down his back. The sweaty-skinned late-July afternoon highlights a clear blue sky, brutally bright hot sun, and temperatures approaching a hundred degrees Fahrenheit. His patch of earth keeps him hidden, but the uncomfortable elements seize all of South Central Maine: too hot in the summer and too cold in the winter.

Sweat pours out, drenching Mack's back and soaking his skin. Chest hair holds up beads of salty moisture. Bloated drops roll down his entire body. Slumping on the black wrought iron patio chair, elbows on the round table, Mack sips his coffee. He towels off and then lights an early-day cigarillo.

The clover-covered front yard attracts the eye, and tree lined meadows across the lane steal his gaze then take his breath. A hundred and seventy years ago, a post–Civil

War village of farmers sat on Mack's eight hundred some acres. Now, buried nearly thirty-five miles into the wilderness from the south side, there is only Mack in his lofted log cabin, and Robin, just up the road.

Shortly after digging in at his hidden paradise, Mack drove down to Portsmouth and plucked his old pal from obscurity. Robin never quite broke away from his miss-stepped youth and existed much as a vagabond. Mack finds him in an old abandoned bus in a mutual friend's farm. The destination banner reads "WEIRD LOAD." Mack hopes the stake here gives Robin the new perspective on life he desperately needs. And Mack is thankful and pleased the needy friend from over forty years before does indeed awaken and reinvent himself.

Other friends are either dead or necessarily out of touch. Mack secretly brings his children in now and then, whenever they want to. They are the only family he has left, but there is no thoughtful repose. Extensive life reviews in early solitude provide insight into exactly what everyone and every event in his life thus far delivered him. There is always something—a message, an understanding, a lesson, some gift that brings promised resolve. A stance with life all about him offers serenity just as things are and why, not how or why things were or might have been.

Ease within a world of synchronicity conveys contentment and toned-down happiness. A simple and positive belief system keeps the past tidily out of mind. Truths of the matter settle nicely inside and obliterate any further presentation of ancient, elderly choice. Steps move forward, and events become elemental lines of continuity on a circular curve.

Snuffing out his small cigar, Mack finishes the last morning mug of coffee and then fills a large covered plastic bottle with ice-cold spring-water. Breathing deep, he stands on the porch, drink in hand, then walks up his driveway.

Embracing the daily hike up the old abandoned logging trail, an in-mind narrative composes and plays improvised poetry, long verses and stanzas. Along his stroll, ground cover, bushes, and trees speak. Happy greetings bless all things encountered—inanimate, living, or dead.

"Hellooooooo." Mack doesn't see Robin. "Neighbor Mack for Robin!" Smoke pipes out the top of Robin's teepee.

"Back here, Mack!" Robin's plot is a mile deeper into the woods than Mack's cabin.

"What's this all about, Robin?" Mack looks

at an aboveground swimming pool and smiles. Robin is a survivalist and endures happily with no electricity and no running water.

"It's a fish pool and hatchery," Robin answers proudly.

"Uh-huh…" Mack wants to hear more. "Okay, explain." He motions Robin to continue.

"I stock it from the pond out back. I keep the largest and smallest fish in the pond for reproduction and growth. The pool is cleansed using natural means, like snails and vegetation and ground-eating fish. Any eggs laid in here eventually spawn fry. I take those babies and put them in the pond."

"Wow." Mack is impressed. "What a great idea!"

"Yeah, well, I found this pool all crumbled up on the roadside and had this idea. I patched it up and assembled it. No leaks!"

"Very good! You are indeed a man who deserves to live in a teepee." Mack and Robin laugh aloud.

"I rented a generator and pump to fill it from the spring. I'll have fresh fish, good eatin' fish, anytime now—soon! I want to share with you."

"Nice! I gratefully accept the offering!"

"Okay. Anytime I miss you on your walkabout and I have some ready, I'll walk it up to your place."

"Sounds great, Robin. Excellent! Thanks, pal."

The poems may transfer over to document or not. Commitment is not high on Mack's directory. Thoughts are tossed aside as he steps from the trail back into his driveway. A creature of need or want, not of habit, crumbs of ideation dance in his mind as his eyes lead to the cabin.

The log house crowns an elevated mound of ledge in a shallow valley at the foot of Sabattus Mountain and the Tacoma Lakes Chain. Solar panels top the 77' × 40' roof, and in his back forty, six immoderately high windmills spin to the wind from the west.

Off the grid…

Mack walks in consoled. He saunters from room to room. Primitive colonial treatment warms him all around. Original art and photographs meet his eye. Downstairs, he picks an album from the eight-thousandth song museum of music and pushes Play. Standing naked in the rec room, he pivots to face a 763-book library—literature, fiction, non-fiction, reference, and a lot of educational textbooks, a fair many written by him. In a trance, under blaring music, he stares at the built-in shelves. He smiles and turns slowly toward the bath and then steps into the cool shower.

Unwelcome thoughts of relationships, or lack thereof, and of his past professional endeavors rarely surface anymore. Mack's power of retention inside a near photographic memory is a curse, but his mind is durable and firm. His journey to success in music and in professional services lie nowhere inside. The absence of haunting replays—all the ways he could have made things better—affords utter tranquility and earned complacency. He thinks, speaks, and resides in the present. Personal pronouns do not clutter his vocabulary: no *I* or *me* and no *you*. And the unwelcome ever-looping musical soundtrack that used to straitjacket his thoughts is thankfully silenced inside his solitary refinement.

2

"Cut it off!"

"Whoa." Patricia wants a retake. "Are you sure, Richard?" She holds out to the side of Richard's head a two-foot ponytail. "Really?"

"Geez, Patricia," Mack struggles with the reasoning. "It is so hot lately. I'm so sweaty. I can't stand it! Sticking to my back, my shoulders, everywhere–ugh! You know?"

"Oh, this is too funny," the salon owner says. "My husband was mowing the lawn this morning. He comes running in here demanding I cut his ponytail off! He said exactly what you just said to me!"

"Well, did you cut it?"

"Richard, he started growing his a relatively short time ago. It wasn't near as long as yours. I mean, you are invested in yours!" She laughs out loud. "This," she declares, again holding up Mack's long ponytail, "this is a twenty-year pony, man!"

"Well?"

"Yes, I cut his. But listen, Richard, " Patricia throws an option out. "I want you to consider this carefully."

"What?" Mack isn't sure where she is headed with this.

"I want you to go home and take three days to reconsider what you think you want today. If you feel the same way three days from now, I will consider your request." She laughs again. "Fair enough?"

"Yes, Patricia. Fair enough."

"Whew. Good." She is genuinely relieved.

"Good suggestion. I'll let you know. For now, why don't I sit here awhile and chat?"

"Of course!"

Mack met Patricia and Robert at a flea market in Hallowell. Characteristically, he struck a conversation with them. He was shopping for wrought iron hardware and punched tin household accessories, still refining the decor after several years there in the house. The couple chatted with him and looked the stuff over, but they were not shopping. Their home is much too contemporary for black iron stuff. Robert and his wife has taken an immediate liking to the friendly older man. He exudes warmth and smiles good nature.

They have learned little about Mack over the years, but that doesn't matter to them. He's very nice and kind. He is retired. He seems to be well-off. He lives alone. He is very intelligent—smart, able to engage in conversation on virtually any topic. He is a one-of-a-kind friend, for sure, unlike the Yankee hillbillies in the Litchfield area. They know nothing of his family or his past, and they share no mutual friends, but that doesn't matter. They like him; he is interesting. And he likes them.

Although Mack detests games, he does sometimes play Trivial Pursuit with them. And he wins. Every time. Few others in or around Litchfield know him, and he keeps Patricia and Robert at a decisive arm's length. Aside from ad hoc, unplanned trips about to the flea market or a monthly trip to the feed and general store, he is usually home. Patricia occasionally invites him to dinner.

Well, that was impulsive now, wasn't it? He has already changed his mind about the haircut. Thank goodness for Patricia's good sense. There is little room for compulsion. He let the heat take hold earlier, and now he feels foolish, but at least he got out. It's been too long.

The ride north is warm, made hot by his leathers, but Mack never rides without protection, and tonight he wears his "known associate" cut. It's an hour-long ride up the smooth highway all the way to Canaan. Then getting off I-95, old State Highway 4 takes him all the way to the clubhouse. Mack arrives first and waits outside twenty minutes before a prospect shows up and unlocks the gate. Fred pulls in as Mack starts his bike.

"Hey, hey, hey, Mr. Mack." The chapter president is his personal motorcycle mechanic. "How's she runnin'?"

"Hey, Fred," Mack is a well-loved benefactor to the club. "Running great, man."

"Let's head in!"

"Right behind you!"

Mack's been riding fifty years. His relationships with the Salem Witches and, later, the Outlaws are far and away decades gone. He's been with the Angels since meeting with the Dade County chapter in Florida. He is patched over in New York and then again relocating to New England. Bikes have always consumed a lifelong alter ego. Bikers are his kind of people. Honest. Free thinkers. No-nonsense. Straight-up. No apologies.

"Okay." Fred puts gavel to table. "Hell's Angels MC Canaan Chapter, third quarter 2029 in session. First off, project status. Spit!"

"Attorney is all over the arrests in Louden. We're all getting off." The table applauds.

Spit continues, "Okay, yeah, I know, huh! All runners—Lewiston/Auburn, Augusta, Waterville, Belfast, Bucksport, and Bangor areas all cashed-in. Zero discrepancy this quarter!"

"Excellent!" Fred bellows. "Next?"

"We are set to provide security for all engagements at Meadowbrook and Limestone.

"We are almost fully in Camden, Bar Harbor, Ellsworth and Newport—solid. Tight. All the way. Pierre and his boys are to be commended. I should have a more precise first readout next quarter, or sooner.

"Finally, we are planning the Toy Run and the Poker Run as we speak. I'll provide an interim readout in three or four weeks. That's it, Cap!"

"Okay, great," Fred continues. "Money! Heh-heh. Fingers, you're up."

"Books balance all around. We absorbed a hit last quarter making bail for the arrestees in Laconia…uh, Louden. There may be additional fines to pay. We'll see. So our club fund is riding a little low by seventy thousand."

"Shit. Right," Fred deadpans. "Hopefully we'll make that up when the newbies pay out. Now, before the breakout meetings, anything else?"

From the front corner of the chapel, Mack raises his hand. "Fred, may I?"

"'Course, bro. Go ahead."

"Happy to share, I've got a contribution of $15,000 for the club this quarter."

"Mack, I'd like to call you king, but I'm the prez!" Fred laughs out loud. "Let's hear it for Mr. Mack, men!"

"My sincere pleasure, guys."

Mack sits on a forest-green fabric futon facing the long log wall opposite him. Legs outstretched, his bare feet rest on a cushion of tightly woven indoor-outdoor carpet. Papers on the end table rattle from the loud oncoming music through the tall skinny Bose speakers.

He listens freely and calmly. Relaxing ground level in the finished daylight basement, the cool downstairs air envelops him refreshingly. No expectations hang in the way of his aloofness. No one ever comes. No one ever will. Besides his children and Robin, no one knows where Mack is or even whether he is alive. He wonders if people ever think about him at all, be it even in the past tense. He turns and sees the taped and battered boxes of cash in the corner. He wants to give it to charity, but action never follows the thought. He sighs. He walks by them every day, never stopping to see. They could open to a gift, or a coffin. He'll give it to his lawyer, ~~John,~~ one day soon.

Amid the audio onslaught, he easily dozes off. Dreams immediately color his subconscious world. It's a vivid abstraction. He is not afraid, but he sweats while taking the beating only a tough-love education can deliver. It's a traveling life out on the blue highways. Street smarts add layers to the already hard shell Mack takes on. But with the accessibility the business offers and the money earned enables, he is caught up in an international subcult of wizards. Hell folds him up to the point of asphyxia. He wakes with a shudder. Though he evidently is no longer on the road, he no doubt remains on the run.

Oh, mother, we enjoy the nighttimes, dreams that frame the adult lives we watch go by—at home, on television, in all their familial glory. We want to need someone and for someone to love us back—regardless of need—no matter what, someone besides mom. Mack wants the need for love, to know love. He tunes his thoughts based on wisdom he gains, so the attributes he commits himself to are what he seeks in a girl, one who can offer to him what he can to her. Tolerance, Mack believes, is a stepping stone to acceptance, if not an impostor-like flaw or cop-out. Acceptance is the answer. So maybe, merely feeling the pain is to know the experience. He smiles with the girls on TV.

This is not private hell. There is no such thing as private hell. Not even in animals. The pack, the others in the colony, grieve for the wounded. Private hell cannot be because every man needs to tell somebody. Someone.

Anyone. No one lives in private hell. They share their world so it will never be private again. The secret must be passed on so that the bearer cannot wallow in depths of self-pity. But we are careful to disregard the empathy of those we trust our secrets with.

No such manufactured or installed cushion exists, but Mack shares his story with his grown children. He tells them, simply-complex, that this is the way it has to be because that is the way it was. Behind his veil resides a cooled, settled lone-wolf lifer. Still, the unclouded skies above him do not equate to an unclouded day.

Stop...stop...STOP.

3

Thriving in a paradise of elite rogue thinkers, Mack falls into his second profession almost by accident. His interest in music-recording technology leads him to wonder about hardware and software that was originally developed for military use, such as data-compression algorithms and large-capacity storage devices. He attends the prestigious Chamberlain Institute for Information Science and finishes a three-year accelerated architect development series in nine months with a perfect score. Mackenzie King is a natural.

The King Consultancy operates in and

around the NYC metro Area. Flourishing on the modern technical theater—something new on the horizon every week—Mack makes big business his business. He becomes known in the megalopolis simply as *King*. Work is bountiful in the condensed, concentrated field. He blows in to the venue, solves technical and managerial problems (their issues), and then blows back out and moves on to another. A golden reputation keeps King Consultancy in high demand. The market is his: he secures wild accomplishment, achievement, and prosperity.

A next-door neighbor in Upper Saddle River is a retired engineer who had worked on the Sidewinder missile program. This neighbor bought Mack a subscription to *Aviation Week* magazine, provoking his interest in additional military-oriented publications, missile defense systems in particular. He becomes self-taught in this area, and at one point, he writes a five-page paper that proposes converting the ship-based antiaircraft Aegis missile into a rudimentary missile defense system. He sends the paper to a California Republican congressman, and his career as a defense consultant begins.

Backed by several influential Capitol Hill lawmakers, Mack receives a series of security clearances so he can work with classified information and covert personnel. In 1992, a Pennsylvania Republican congressman, then the chairman of the House Military Research and Development Subcommittee, nominates Mackenzie King to chair the Civilian Advisory Board for Ballistic Missile Defense.

Mack's work with that panel leads to consulting contracts with the Pentagon's Missile Defense Agency and National Geospatial-Intelligence Agency. He consults to the US Department of Defense and the US intelligence community, as well as for defense-oriented manufacturers, including Science Applications International Corporation, Northrop Grumman Corp., General Dynamics, and General Atomics Aeronautical Systems Inc.

He's quoted in industry periodicals as saying his unconventional approach to thinking about terrorism, tied to his interest in technology, is a major reason he became sought after by the government:

"We thought turntables were for playing records until rappers began to use them as instruments, and we thought airplanes were for carrying passengers until terrorists realized they could be used as missiles. My big thing is to look toward the future, but also at existing technologies and try to see other ways they can be used, which happens in music all the time and happens to be what terrorists are incredibly good at."Mack appears in public debates and as a guest on major cable news outlets, such as CNN and Fox News, advocating missile defense. He serves as a national spokesman for Americans for Missile Defense, a coalition of organizations devoted to the issue. He is listed as *senior thinker and raconteur* at the Institute for Human and Machine Cognition. It is in this capacity that he is lassoed into the Fellowship for Advanced Energy Discovery–Think Tank.

The cell phone vibrates on Mack's desk, making that familiar buzzing sound against the wood as it shimmies toward the table's edge. He looks at the humming device but does not answer. The contractual elements of his upcoming engagements and scanning the pile of 1099 forms from previous placements take all his attention. His initial term for business contracts is ninety days. Extensions are optional at either end: the host company may opt in or not, and Mack has the same opportunity.

Mack is signed with the Chamberlain Institute Technical Resources–Professional Services Agency. The company handles placement and all the other line-item specifics of the jobs presented to Mack. It makes the clerical aspect of Mack's job much easier. Upon agreement, the agency offers Mack employment in the subcontractor category.

The institute Mack once attended approaches him about a professorship there. As an independent contractor, Mack commands a $1,500-a-day salary before deductions. Teaching two nights a week and every other Saturday add another $2,250 every seven days. He accepts the offer.

Although the institute agency promises jobs nine months out, Mack offers to sign off on each assignment singularly forty-five days in advance. He has many business contacts that prefer to work with him directly, which means more money to Mack and less out-of-pocket for the employer.

IBM aggressively courts Mack King to the point of irritation, urging him to sign over to exempt employee status. He has much history subcontracting with Big Blue, and they would like him to get onboard, or at least sign longer contracts. He reviews and makes his determination every sixty days. Procuring work is sometimes difficult, what with so many headhunters knocking at his door. Mack is a textbook Libra—decisions are tough in coming.

He looks down at his phone and sees the little red prompt on the phone icon. He is so involved with his business that he forgot all about the missed call. He opens the phone app and sees the caller left a voice mail message. The number is not hidden but is not in his contacts, so he doesn't know who it is; but out of curiosity, he listens.

"Hello, Mr. King," the message begins, "my name is Sanjay Ganesh. I am the designee in charge of recruiting high-tech scientists and engineers for a special project sanctioned by the International Energy Commission led by the United States. I would like to arrange a meeting with you to tell you more about the project and gauge your interest in joining the team. Please call me back to discuss. Thank you, Mr. King."

Mack performs several Internet searches but finds no references anywhere to an "International Energy Commission." Rather than discourage him, this actually piques his interest. He returns the call and speaks to Mr. Ganesh. They decide to meet the night after at the high-end "manor" in West Orange.

Over an exquisite private dinner, Mack learns the framework of the project, but it is the objective that astounds him. It appears to be born of big oil and that an official in the Pentagon anonymously submitted Mack's name for consideration on the exclusive cream-of-the-crop team. The work is highly classified, and any participation in it is shrouded in multilayered security and confidentiality. Mack agrees to follow the protocol.

Having reported to several generals and chiefs of staff, the classification of this new project does not faze Mack. He listens to Mr. Ganesh intently, recognizing that the young man can only take the conversation so far before reaching his censored limit of topics.

—❦ **4** ❧—

The long black car sent for Mack stops and starts. Interstate 287 is congested, as usual. He sits back on the plush leather bench seat and sips on a bottle of water. He's no less frustrated regardless of who's driving: it's an effort to kick back and enjoy the ride like he is supposed to do in a limo!

"We're here," the driver announces.

"So White Plains, huh?" Mack asks.

"Yes, sir. We are in White Plains, New York."

The stone-sided town house is in a gated hamlet. Each house sits on a private three-acre lot. The driver helps carry Mack's suitcases and bags inside. Tile, wood, and opal Berber floors, brushed stainless steel appliances, and microfiber furniture are brand-new. The exact style of stuff Mack likes. Mack peeks in the refrigerator.

"And how far is this from the lab?" Mack asks.

"Twenty minutes, sir. Pickup is at nine-thirty tomorrow morning."

"Excellent. I'll be ready!"

"Is there is anything you want or need before I go for the night?" he asks, handing Mack the key ring to the house.

"The fridge looks stocked, and everything else appears to be in place—just fine. Thank you."

"White Plains is in Westchester County, New York," Mack reads the Wikipedia entry for the city. It is the county seat and commercial hub of Westchester, an affluent suburban county, home to a million people, just north of New York City.

It is located in south-central Westchester, with its downtown about seven miles east of the Hudson River and seven miles northwest of the Long Island Sound. It is bordered to the north by the town of North Castle, to the north and east by the village of Harrison, to the south by the town of Scarsdale, and to the west by the town of Greenburgh. He is on Old Mamaroneck Road, which is not too far a cry from Saddle River. The area is rustic, artsy, colonial. Yes, it's nice here. He studies the map and sits back in the desk chair. Okay, then.*In case I get lost, I know where I am!*The town house is clean—like new. Everything has a vibrant air about it. The appliances give off a cool matte shine, the furniture is comfortable, and the floors are welcoming to the foot. Mack sets up his laptop on the small oak living-room desk in the corner facing outward—feng shui, you know. There is a tower-style desktop device on the larger desk in the office, a sunny alcove off the living room. The fridge is well stocked according to the wishes he relayed to Ganesh. He is delighted with the music system and television monitor. It is a single ground-floor home—but expansive.

Mack unpacks his suitcases and bags into the dresser, bureau, and closet. His jackets go in the closet off the entry foyer. Sitting in the office, he logs in to the project server and establishes his credentials, a onetime-only task. The project folders and systems are locked down until tomorrow. Watching the local PBS station before heading to bed, Mack enjoys roasted pepper humus over Stoned Wheat crackers.

Mack is ready by 9:15 a.m., and his car arrives right on time. He steps into the black high-class Mercedes sedan and lays his brown Coach satchel on the seat next to him. Along the way to the lab, woods line the road that fronts the Mamaroneck River. Looking out the windows along the way is a pleasant and relaxing surprise. Mack sits back without any specific thought.

"Nice ride, huh?" Mack says to the driver.

"It's a very nice area, Mr. King."

"Hey, please call me Mack. And I'd rather not call you *driver…*"

"My name is Jools."

"Ah, old English!" *What a great name!* Mack smiles.

"Yes. I have a dual citizenship."

"Very good then, Jools."

"We're here," Jools says.

"Where...exactly?"

"Sleepy Hollow," Jools replies with a wide smile. He sees Mack's expression in the rearview mirror. "Yes. Sleepy Hollow."

Mack saw Sleepy Hollow on an area map last night. It is a ten-mile ride, but the driveway into the work site is another six minutes in itself. It zigzags up a slope the way mountain roads do. The building is an arc-shaped structure, like a fallen parenthesis, about twelve stories high. The convex side represents the front of the remarkable structure. The exterior is black mirrored glass. Mack assumes they are windows.

"Gotta love that!" Mack points to the building and smiles as he climbs out of the car. "Quite a place."

"Indeed it is."

"Wow."

"See you tonight," Jools says as Mack walks away.

Bag slung over his shoulder, Mack steps slowly up the walkway to the entrance. There is an armed uniformed guard standing outside.

"May I see your identification, sir?"

"Yes. Sure."

There is a team of security professionals inside the double doors. It's like entering a courthouse. Mack empties his pockets and walks through the electronic gauntlet. He stops at reception where he is asked to sign in and wait for his host. An impeccably dressed statuesque red-auburn-haired woman comes through the wooden doors to his left.

"Ah, Mr. King!"

"Yes, ma'am."

"So happy you are here." Her clothes are tailored to fit like a colorful coating of fabricated skin. Mack is quite taken. "I am Joan, floor management"

"Nice to meet you," Mack replies. "You know my name." He chuckles.

"Are your quarters up to standard, sir?"

"Yes, yes, everything is fine. Very nice. I like the place a lot. Thank you."

She hands him a card. "Call me anytime for anything. It is my job to make sure you remain happy and comfortable while on this project. Home and office, lab." A radiant smile frames perfect white teeth.

"Thank you very much. Good deal." Yes. Mack likes Joan already.

"Follow me, then, Mr. King."

She points out different rooms of interest as they walk down a long hallway–private break room, team break room, restrooms, and vending area. The mail room is downstairs. Clerical offices are upstairs. There is also a full-size cafeteria with their own chef and caterer.

"Here we are. These doors lead to your labs. Here is your SecurID. It gets you everywhere you need to go inside. Please carry it with you at all times and try not to lose it." Joan smiles and blushes.

"Okay, Joan, thanks. Understood."

"This is as far as I go for now, Mr. King."

"Oh. Okay."

"Your project manager will greet you on the other side." Joan smiles as she turns to walk away.

Mack holds his ID to the reader, places his

palm over the hand reader, and then looks into the retina scan. After a series of loud clicks under a humming sound, the door slowly opens. Mack pictures a multilocked loft in Greenwich Village and of Maxwell Smart and smiles.

He steps through the thick glass doors, and the second set opens for him automatically. Another uniformed officer stands at the ready.

"Good morning, sir." The guard smiles.

"Morning." Mack smiles back.

"Mr. Al Kahtani will be here in a moment."

"Thank you."

An Arab man approaches from thirty yards beyond. He nears and extends his right hand out toward Mack. "Hello, sir. Isaak Al Kahtani."

"Ah, Mr. Al Kahtani. Nice to meet you. Mackenzie King."

"We are very excited to have you here on the team." He motions gracefully for Mack to follow.

"Pleasure is mine, Mr. Al Kahtani." He and Isaak stride ahead.

"Pleased with your residence, Mr. King? Sleep well?"

"Very. Yes. Thank you very much."

They stop at a set of thick wooden doors. Al Kahtani holds his badge to the scanner, and Mack follows him through. The world opens up to a glass menagerie of office space, where each office, library, conference room, and laboratory lie distinctly laid out before them. Every space is a fishbowl style. Mack saw this layout floor model only once before, at M&M Mars-ISI in Hackettstown.

"Here are our offices and labs, Mr. King."

"I clearly see that." Mack looks at Al Kahtani and softly laughs.

"It is a ground-up dedication to transparency." Al Kahtani laughs.

"Thankfully, there are no mazelike pathways between each large cubicle," Mack says then adds, "I've worked in similar environments. I like it, all right."

"Good! I'll show you around. Then we'll all meet together over coffee."

5

There are nameplates at every seat around the fine cherry conference table. Mack sits at his place and waits. One by one, the other team members arrive. Al Kahtani introduces himself to the group, offers a brief background statement, and asks they do the same. He gestures to the individual team members one by one.

"Benjamin Hall, Texas Oil Drilling teammate at Sleepy Hollow Think Tank."

"Mackenzie King, United States, Science of Ballistic Trajectory and System Technology at Sleepy Hollow Think Tank."

"Charlize Laherrère, French robotics/ petroleum engineer teammate at Sleepy Hollow Think Tank." (Robotics includes the branches of mechanical and electrical engineering and computer science.)"Omar El-Mofty, Arabian economist teammate at Sleepy Hollow Think Tank."

"William Cooper, American automobile consultant at Sleepy Hollow Think Tank."

The team members share greetings and chat over coffee, bagels, pastries, and fruit. Mack is happy everyone speaks English. Charlize's accent is cute as all get-out.

"Please, everyone. Let us continue now," Al Kahtani calls out. "A few ground rules, if you will. Everyone holds at least one doctorate degree, but I'd like us to address each other by surname. I wish to work within equality. This offers the most respect given our varied backgrounds, heritage, and individuality and, in our case, leaves no ambiguity. You may call me Kahtani. Don't worry about the *Al*."I have name tags for each of you, but as soon as we're comfortable with each other's names, feel free to go without. We will meet every morning right here at 9:50 a.m. for a status and planning readout. Anyone can call a meeting as they deem necessary. I oversee. However, you are all responsible for interproject coordination. All I need are copies from the scribe.

"Each of you team leaders are responsible for all project/task-related documentation. I have assigned each of you your own technical writer, but you'll have to provide specs and source stock as necessary. We share an executive administrator. I'll bring her around for introductions.

"All six of us—counterparts—will spend our first seven months researching 'energy harvesting' given the target locales. The deliverable is a proven feasibility study and dependent conceptual model. The following six months, we will produce the logical model. All of you will, at that time, build your own teams to support oncoming detailed tasks. I won't take us any further at this point in time.

"You will find on your desks a packet including building layout, fire escape route, phone extensions, and a team member cross-reference. Also, find our list of best practices, project scope, project breakdown, and phase-respective functional specifications. Do you have questions so far?"

"Are the log-in credentials in the info packet?" Cooper asks. The team looks over at Kahtani.

"Oh yes, of course," Kahtani answers. "I failed to mention that. You'll find them right up front in the packet. Thank you. Anyone else?

"Today is designated a time to make acquaintance—with each other and with the systems you'll be working with.

"Now then, ongoing, shall we plan a forty-eight-hour workweek? That's four twelve-hour workdays per week."

"I think that is a marvelous idea, Kahtani," Mack responds. "How about you all?"

All around the table agree on the work schedule.

"All right," the project manager continues, "you may take either Friday or Monday off—decided among yourselves. Let's loosely plan work hours daily for nine in the morning till seven in the evening."

"Yes, sir!" the table resounds.

Mack adds, "I suggest Fridays off so we get four-day Holiday weekends."

"All right, then, understand that our work schedule is dictated by all of us, erring on our project status. So now, partners...behold the fellowship for Energy Discovery Think Team!"

"Aye, aye! Hear, hear!"

"Finally, for this morning...although this may go without saying, it is imperative that I reiterate its importance. This entire project, all involved, and the activities of our evolving team are considered highly classified and must remain veiled in secrecy. That means here and your quarters. All understood?"

"Excuse me, Mr. King?" Joan gently interrupts with a soft knock on the open door.

"Of course, Joan." Mack smiles at the attractive redhead. "Please come in."

"Thank you. I have a message from Mr. Al Kahtani. He asks that the team review the scope definition in your packet in time to review at lunch today."

"Okay. I saw this coming." Mack grins.

"Oh, good. Then please join us in the team conference room for a special catered, working lunch." She gives Mack a knowing smirk.

"I will do that. What time?"

"Oh yes, twelve-thirty."

"Great! I look forward to seeing you in a little bit." And he means it.

Waterfall methodology is historically the most used across all industries, and it is very common in software development and construction, even within other more modern techniques. Mack knows there are many versions of the waterfall method, but the rudimentary includes the high-level phases: request for project, feasibility study, requirements specification, design, construction, integration testing and debugging, installation, and maintenance.

Inside feasibility, Mack notes that project motivation is essential to establish a firm foundation of purpose that is based on agreed-upon fundamentals and will generate the commitment of resources necessary to attract private investment, both project development capital and project finance capital, into Advanced Energy projects.

Initial project-assessment documents risk assessment and potential fatal flaws, such as issues of site, resource, offtake, and the related issues of economics and bankability. Mack understands that high-level assessment of the subject areas—with the purpose of identifying fatal flaws, significant areas of risk, and gaps of information—constitute the indelible deliverable.

Incremental investment decisions must be made at crucial intervals within the feasibility study. With the assessment conducted, the team determines what has been learned and, using the output of a pro forma from economic analysis, advise if sufficient motivation exists to continue forward with an incremental investment or not. If the project sponsors and financiers agree that motivation exists, they direct investments to most efficiently take the project forward to the next decision point.

Investment of more time and resources in predevelopment work more fully produces information, concentrating on the incremental investment suggested by the prior iteration. The team concentrates on verifying site, resource, and offtake elements while continually seeking fatal flaws in permit, technology, team, and capital, pursuing mitigating actions for risks across the project.

The second assessment conducted, considering what has been learned and the output of the pro forma economic analysis, documents if sufficient motivation exists to continue forward with an incremental investment. At this point, Mack notes his understanding and points out that it should be obvious that site conditions, resource, and offtake arrangements are absolutely bankable and economic.

They have to produce a framework project plan and models that address and define known elements about the project. It is used in preparation for delivery to the backers in a potential procurement or RFP, request for project, phase. References and documentation of the existing status in hand must be sufficient for developers to assess remaining risks and development activity, as well as provide an undimmed and defined pathway to final approval and contract execution.

Based on the assessment of the output project plan for RFP, a "go forward/stop" decision is made. The project needs to be judged to include acceptable and financeable risks by the financiers' development community. They may use industry interaction or advisory as a reference to establish criteria.

The sponsors typically pursue private partners through the RFP process. Their representatives conduct a competitive procurement of the project, acknowledging the continued development process and agreement to work as an active transaction partner to pursue project completion.

*So much for classified secrecy.*However, selection and negotiation with an awardee is not necessary for this project. The team in Sleepy Hollow *are* the implant qualified, selected, negotiated, and awarded recipients of the opportunity. With the ongoing support of resources, for the development of the project to carry it forward into a completed deal mutually beneficial to both parties, ongoing partnerships will and must actively participate.

"Good afternoon! I am glad you were all able to attend," Kahtani welcomes the team. They nod. "As a warming for you all, there is a surf 'n' turf dinner with all the sides. There are also vegetarian and vegan cuisine choices."

The long table adjacent to the back short wall is dressed for a gourmet buffet-style offering. All the hot and cold line choices are elegantly labeled. Maine lobster, wagyu ribeye steak, Jersey Silver Queen sweet corn, complex tossed salad—the food line seems to last forever. Joan has not missed a thing.

"Please eat and enjoy. We'll have a brief meeting afterward."

"I have something on the lighter side," Laherrère chimes in.

"Please." Kahtani extends his hand, palm up. "Go ahead, Mademoiselle Laherrère."

"That's just it, everyone. My name. You all have surnames that roll off the tongue. Easy to say, but mine is wonky. I'd like you all to please call me Charlie. Is that okay, Kahtani?"

"Of course! If you insist, then I second it. Consider it done!" He chuckles. "Charlie! So here is our lineup:

Dempsey, Kahtani, King, Hall, Charlie, Mofty, and Cooper. Are we set?" Kahtani asks.

"Yes, sir!" the team replies in unison.

"Did you all have an opportunity to review our preproject scope? Are there questions?"

Mack speaks up. "The steps within scope make sense, boilerplate, but there is no reference, even a hint, as to what we are actually scoping out."

"That is true, Mr. King." Kahtani takes a deep breath. "Everyone, please take this afternoon to review the executive summary, background, and the introduction. Take the rest of the week to learn the navigation points inherent within the systems we will use. Addressing Mr. King's question, we'll delve into project specifics on Monday."

Mack reads on. He feels the furtiveness of the project, the residences, and the work site, along with the vague project management documentation odd, provocative and enthralling, intriguing. The development of renewable energy generation projects has become attractive to a variety of energy consumers, installations and large institutions, land and real estate owners, and others who recognize the economic, environmental, and security potential of renewable energy, as slow as they are permitted and commercial they've become: green, even by label, brand. "Green."

This summary introduces a seemingly similar project that will have delivered advanced energy techniques instead. The aspiration for this project, and regardless of whether the host will ultimately finance and build the project out themselves, embeds itself in the role of project developer in the early stages of project development. The size and diversity of potential project sponsors is significant given the subject: advanced energy.

Mack can think of many candidates and types them up as he thinks of them, including but not limited to, the federal government and the military, including all its agencies and departments, facilities and installations; public and private universities and colleges; local and state governments; tribal nations; private and public companies from sole proprietorships to Fortune 500 companies; real estate investment trusts to private individuals; nonprofits and nongovernmental organizations.

In his experience, it is rare to have resident a well-versed professional energy project development experience within the vast majority of these new market participants. Many have largely dealt with the gamut of energies by simply paying the bill. But now—here—they are motivated to consider the relatively radical change of producing their own by virtue of this project, and by at least boring into and participating in the project in some meaningful way.

Mack begins to understand that project development in this case is primarily viewed as an entrepreneurial activity and is subject to significant risks and unknowns while requiring ongoing investment of time, financial, and even political resources toward output that consists of a completed project.

The document thus far reads referentially as preparation or preproduction. Prior to embarking on the specifics, it is essential to gauge the fundamental market characteristics that create the conditions for success and provide sufficient support to generate the necessary "project motivation." A motivated project, Mack knows, is one that has a free pathway to success and enough opportunity that it simply cannot be ignored.

We can't afford not to do it.

This project, apparently, is driven by some baseline need or interest in completing the project, the fundamental economics of energy in the interested areas, existing policy environment, available commercial technologies, and virtually limitless resources. Mack sees something here that bears obvious affinity to the project scope he read earlier. Development risk and fatal flaws absolutely need to be identified, managed, and analyzed quickly and accurately to conserve capital resources.

Once project motivation is plainly established and communicated with purpose and confidence, Mack can seriously envision more than one approach to this specific project. The first incremental investment in the project is worthwhile and necessary: it will have become immediately coherent that all expenditures are subject to the risk of complete loss, and this risk must be recognized and managed. Mack adds a margin note:

Identify risk should the SUCCESSFUL *project conclude with implementation.*

Mack sits back and sips on his ice water. *The project is not about renewable energy; it is, instead, as it is named, about advanced energy.*

This implies something far exceeding any perceived energy exploration today. Mack would have guessed something that involves extraterrestrial harvesting, but the skill sets employed herein do not suggest space in any way unless they plan to tap him into that concept.

Let's see:

Kahtani, project and team-related questions, concerns, and communication, including scope, deliverables; reporting up and conveying down;

Hall, drilling system design, detailed application, testing and planning;

King, ballistic trajectory, detonation, impact and recovery system design, detailed application, testing and planning;

Charlie, robotics, mechanical, electronic system and mobile design, detailed application, testing and planning;

Mofty, project cost estimates, detailed cost definition, and overall economic management and reporting;

Cooper, mobile vehicular design, build-out, and oversight; and

Joan Dempsey, office setup and moves; telephone updates; office supplies; general site and office-related questions, concerns, and requests; personal quarters-related requests.

Mack documents that two concepts need to be developed—project motivation and the project development environment. Each team member will have to highlight and support the predevelopment and development processes and activities with respect to their expertise.

The first deliverable is project motivation: a motivated project is one that bears strong basis to come to fruition. It is built on economics and risks that are acceptable to all parties, supportive policies, an execution pathway, and project bankability. Mack documents his five essential areas for strong project motivation—baseline, economics, policy, technology, and consensus.

"Yes, Mr. King?"

"Mr. Al Kahtani," Mack begins, "I understand this project is classified in every sense of the word."

"Yes?"

"Well, our sponsor's and stakeholder's identity is nonexistent in the feasibility guide. Their respective offices are vaguely documented at best."

"That is correct," Al Kahtani confirms and smiles.

Mack looks into Al Kahtani's eyes, reads his deadpan expression, and after a few seconds, continues, "We were groomed to accept the covertness and classification of the project, and me of all people comprehend and accept the importance. However, our own secret inclusion in the team suggests that we, or I, speaking for myself, might be privy to any raw data and produced information that lends itself to project management and success."

"I fully understand. Go on."

"Many times, especially in the early phases of project definition—feasibility studies and motivation building—analysts become better enabled to produce more meaningful and satisfying deliverables when they are aware of the decision makers' position, perspective, and mind-set toward, or even disposition from, the project as a whole." Mack takes a deep breath.

"Of course." Kahtani clears his throat. "Of course, I do understand your concern and your point, especially considering your specific contributions to the project. You'd be better armed with more ammunition, right?" Al Kahtani chuckles.

"Precisely, sir."

"Mr. King, please take this at my word, and let us suffice it to say that project sponsorship is already on board and see this phase as a way to *disprove*, rather than approve, the plans based on your team's delivery."

"Oh." Mack takes a moment to absorb what he's hearing. "I see. So, motivation is not the more deciding aspect of the deliverable, but risk is?"

"You may say that. So, Mr. King, this particular question of sponsor identity is left open at this point in time, that is, until or when the answers become ever essential to project success, even paramount, if you will."

"." Mack is fine with the explanation, but he's compelled to close it up from his end. "Although I am quite at ease, the team sees this as a bit queer. So I've heard. However, I am certain we can deliver the goods, motivation and budget, and the risks, no matter how generic or vanilla with regard to the audience."

"Thank you for challenging the baseline, Mr. King. But working alongside you and the team, I am positively confident. I have rock-solid faith, in you particularly."

7

It's so quiet and so peaceful. No highway turbulence; no loud sounds of children running through the streets, and absent too the red-and-blue sirens that forever wail in the New Jersey nights. Soft white noise slips in from the breeze outside and the flow of the Mamaroneck River. Mack points the remote control at the television and presses a button that obliterates the stillness.

He pauses at a channel presenting a documentary about renewable energy. The project—yes, so it's not about renewable energy: it is about advanced energy. What the heck is that? Is he to define what that is, *advanced energy*? What? Is he supposed to build upon existing technological methods? He watches the show, listens, and takes notes.

With wind power, airflows are used to run wind turbines. The wind is a function of the cube of the wind speed, so as wind speed increases, power output increases up to the maximum output for the particular turbine. Areas where winds are stronger and more constant, such as offshore and high-altitude sites, are preferred locations for wind farms.

Globally, the long-term technical potential of wind energy is believed to be five times total current global energy production, or forty times current electricity demand, assuming all practical barriers are overcome. This would require wind turbines to be installed over massively large areas, particularly in areas of higher wind resources, such as offshore.

In 2018, wind generated only 3 percent of the world's total electricity. And even turbine power is under attack from activists over the slaughter of winged creatures of the earth. Logistic concerns obviously present, considering long distance delivery of wind-powered electricity.

Hydropower—energy in water—can be harnessed and used. Since water is about eight hundred times denser than air, even a slow flowing stream of water or moderate sea swell, can yield considerable amounts of energy. There are many forms of water energy, such as hydroelectric energy, which is a term usually reserved for large-scale hydroelectric dams; microhydro systems, which are hydroelectric power installations that typically produce up to a miserly one hundred kilowatts of power.

They are often used in water-rich areas as a remote area power supply. Run-of-the-river hydroelectricity systems derive kinetic energy from rivers without the creation of a large reservoir.

Yet there ever seems to be activists' arguments against large-scale hydroelectric dams. What about wave power? That is one of two advanced type of hydropower that is not being exploited today. Wave power captures the energy of ocean surface waves and tidal power, converting the energy of tides. Ocean thermal energy conversion uses the temperature difference between cooler deep and warmer surface waters. Neither have economic feasibility today. Activists shun anything manipulative.

Solar energy, radiant light and heat from the sun, is harnessed using a range of ever-evolving technologies such as solar heating, photovoltaics, concentrated solar power, solar architecture, and artificial photosynthesis. Solar technologies are broadly characterized as either passive solar or active solar depending on the way they capture, convert, and distribute solar energy.

Passive solar techniques include orienting a building to the sun, selecting materials with favorable thermal mass or light-dispersing properties, and designing spaces that naturally circulate air. Active solar technologies encompass solar thermal energy, using solar collectors for heating, and solar power—converting sunlight into electricity either directly using photovoltaics or indirectly using concentrated solar power.

There are still no concrete best practices methods or even best hardware implementations to capture, store, and convert solar potential. The universal solution is not even close *to reality; there are always too many new things on the horizon. The job is never quite done. How ironic.*Geothermal energy is from thermal energy generated and stored in the earth. Thermal energy is the energy that determines the temperature of matter. Earth's geothermal energy originates from the original formation of the planet and from radioactive decay of minerals. The heat that is used for geothermal energy comes from deep within the earth all the way down to its core—four thousand miles down.

At the core, temperatures may reach over nine thousand degrees Fahrenheit. Heat conducts from the core to surrounding rock. Extremely high temperature and pressure cause some rock to melt, which is commonly known as magma. Magma convects upward since it is lighter than the solid rock. This magma then heats rock and water in the crust, sometimes up to seven hundred degrees Fahrenheit. From hot springs, geothermal energy has been used for bathing since Paleolithic times and for space heating since ancient Roman times, but it is now better known for electricity generation.

This source for ever-ready energy doesn't even pass the straight face test. Would anybody really seriously consider probing four-thousand miles into the earth's core? All across the earth?

Biomass is biological material derived from living, or recently living, organisms. It most often refers to plants or plant-derived materials. As an energy source, biomass can either be used directly via combustion to produce heat or indirectly after converting it to various forms of biofuel.

*Ah.*Mack sits up in his chair.

This, this could really go somewhere. Biomass energy, the planet fix.

Having designed and developed every category of information technology system and application, it's easy for Mack to learn the project systems from a user's perspective. He's not sure how the others feel about it, but he is quite satisfied with the user interfaces and background functionality. The systems are intuitive, intelligent, and wildly powerful. Mack is not often impressed, but he is now, sitting at his desk in Sleepy Hollow.

"Good morning all!" Kahtani greets the team. "And happy Monday. Anyone did anything interesting over weekend?"

"I went over to Hell's Kitchen on Saturday," Mack replies. "Didn't buy anything, except a fine meal, but I love to browse the market there. I stayed in on Sunday."

"I flew home Friday night," Hall yawns. "Excuse me, just got in this morning."

"Likewise," Cooper says. "And I am ready to work!"

"Excellent, gentlemen.

We shall concentrate this week on motivation and risk assessment. Please document your deliverables with respect to your area of expertise, but no further. If you do have thoughts relevant to some other area, then please note them separate from your deliverable and pass it to the appropriate designee. We will use those lists to charge a discussion to follow that of our deliverable rollout. Let's plan on Friday morning."

"The document templates are in a subdirectory within the Project Management folder," Joan says. "They are named logically and in order of logical sequence. Just a reminder."

"And as always," Kahtani adds, "you may add anything relevant to your deliverable to the document but do not subtract anything from it.

Before setting out on a week-long endeavor, I wish to cover two key areas of interests. You asked for this information last week, and I promised I'd deliver it today.

"First, overall sponsorship of the project falls under the World Global Warming Federation, the US Department of Energy—Office of Scientific and Technical Information—US Department of Commerce and the National Technical Information Service. Naturally, there are line item identifiers for the multitude of actors within each of those three departments, federations. I have updated all project management files appropriately. Please add the three of these to your docs."

"May I ask how the individuals marry to this project?" Mack asks. "The project they intend to sponsor?"

"I have a cross-reference, project management addendum attached to all deliverables that require atomic sponsor identification," Kahtani says. "This complies with the classification protocol."

"Makes our lives simpler!" Cooper laughs.

"Now." Kahtani breathes deep. "I have unlocked a project charter, project definition, and project statement. They further define scope, objectives, and participants of our project. They provide a preliminary delineation of roles and responsibilities, outlines the project objectives, identifies the main stakeholders, and defines the authority of the project manager. They serve as a reference of authority for the future of the project. Please Sticky Note or yellow comment as you see fit. I'll review regularly.

You should familiarize yourselves with the documentation." Kahtani continues, "but I am going to outline the objective to you all right now. That way, I can answer all your immediate questions before we go any further. Are we good?"

This is what they hunger for, what they need. The scientists nod and express knowing affirmation.

"Thank you, team." Kahtani prepares the terse wording he practiced the night before. "Energy production and consumption have become keen topics in the scientific and the activist's world. Whereas most everybody agrees that clean renewable energy should remain the ultimate goal, we also know that something must be done more immediately to break the stronghold the world's enemies have around traditional energy production: oil."

He reads.

"This team, our team, has been sanctioned to deliver on two primary objectives: (1) w

here to find virtually limitless supplies and

(2) how to extract the raw material and get it to the refineries.

The motivation and risk assessment due must also document high-level answers or options to those two requirements. So how are we—?"

"This is exactly what we were hoping to get, Kahtani." Mack speaks right up. "Now it makes sense."

"I need not remind you of the sensitive nature of the project. But I feel compelled to divulge this: hard delivery of locale and methodologies decided upon, and the course we will have taken, will always remain highly classified. Everything we do, team, from beginning to end regarding this project is secret. We are a secret society here in the Sleepy Hollow labs.

We are close to operations manufacturing, so keep that to the forefront too as that time approaches."

Mack's $1.5 million salary per project phase is almost two times what his consultancy brings home in a year. The government contract is bound to five years, with a $1 million sign-on extension every project phase. He stands to make well over $11.5 million by the time the project closes, less than five years from now.

No mind on the money, Mack has "advanced energy" on his mind at bedtime. if the project had anything to do with renewable energy harvesting, there would be no need for any classified think tank to kick off a secret project. Existing transparent, commercially specialized initiatives would already be hard at work on it. And, of course, they are under the watchful eyes of clean energy groups and renewable energy activists around the world—feeding the unknowing by the spoonful.

Mack is no expert on energy harvesting, but he knows enough to ask himself the focused and necessary questions. We purchase raw oil from abroad—foreign continents. We harvest oil, gas, coal, and shale across country and within our water rights. We must refine our own oil also through big oil companies.

Harvesting virtually all our energy resources goes through big business. So even though there is harvesting within our country, we still have to buy it from the oil companies and refineries.

Where have we not looked? What have we not done?

He begins a stub document. The term *advanced* suggests the scope of the project builds up from or expands upon existing raw forms of material and already established energy sources. What do we harvest currently? Oil, gas, coal, and shale. Where do we get them? Drill sites and mines. The same two operators bubble to the top: what and where. The one ever-present descriptor is some form of undercover. Mack polishes up the one-pager and calls a meeting.

"I submit this booster to the team," Mack begins. "And ask only for the time to brainstorm based on the contents." He places a separate sheet of paper face down on the table in front of him.

Kahtani leaves the team to work the day in their meeting room. He is happily impressed and grateful for Mr. King. The team finishes reading the paper and sits, hands clasped on the table staring at Mack.

"Okay," Mack says, smiling. "Read it through again once more, please."

They look at each other and then back at him. Hall shrugs his shoulders and asks, "King, come on. Why?"

"Yeah," Cooper says. "It's four paragraphs, man. I think we get it."

Mack leans on the head of the table with his hands, glaring at the others. And he speaks through his teeth like Clint Eastwood."Entertain me, please. We are a team, are we not? Or do you have something else you have to attend to?"

The team falls silent, reads, and then they look to Mack for a cue. "Thank you. Now, what strikes you overall about the content therein?"

"Nothing we don't already know." Hall deadpans.

"All right then, Hall. In three words or less, what stands out?"

"Come on, King."

"Hall!" Mack will drive this train. "There are no wrong answers! Now, do it, please!"

"Extremely simple," Hall answers. "Okay? Simple."

"Yeah," Cooper says. "Simple."

"Excellent!" It's the answer Mack is looking for. "See that? You got it!"

"What is this, King?" Cooper wants to know.

"I outlined the problem. The consensus is that it is simple. The solution I have in mind is not included in the document. Let's take down our shields and open up for an interview-style brainstorm.

"Okay," Hall says."I submit to you that there is no confidence in further surface drilling, etcetera, of the earth. What say you?"

The team agrees, seconds, and accepts the submission.

"Good. We'll keep that right here in front of us but move on for now." Mack directs. "Next question: Is there likely any other material in the earth besides what we already mine from atop or near so?"

"How are we to know?" Charlie asks.

"I am comfortable with contributions based

on 'what we know thus far,'" Mack says. "I can ask for no more." He smiles at Charlie.

Answers are not jumping forth from the team, so Mack puts the assumption out there on the table. "It's fair to say that no material beyond gas, oil, coal, and shale exists for the taking from just below the earth's crust. We have no 'reserves.' Agreed?"

Mack almost jumps with a start when the entire team serves him a unanimous "Yes!"

"Great! It is seconded that there is no confidence in harvesting from the surface of the earth. The team also agrees that no material beyond limited or restricted oil, coal, gas, and shale exists for the taking from the earth.

"Let us take that backwards." Mack facilitates. "Name a location offering secrecy but at the same time provides suitable surface area on which to operate.

Is there an oil-rich place not yet discovered or tapped?

What material can we expect to find—based on present-day excursions?

"Going beyond present-day state-of-the-art unearthing guarantees a challenging operation, but not necessarily implausible. Be that as it may, the endgame, the product, the essence of the project is unabashedly elementary."

Mack reads from the document. "One preliminary finding based on factors listed is that surface discovery, drilling or mining is disqualified. Another assumption is that we have no evidence or reason to believe that any material beyond oil, coal, gas, and shale exists. Additionally, it goes to say that any further discovery lies not on terrestrial surface or above sea level."

Mack continues.

"I suggest we look at the definition of *surface* and *terrestrial*. Finally, we are not tasked to discover new material as much as we are a way to harvest it. Therefore, we consider the term *advanced*. Please discuss as a group for five minutes."

Hall complains as the rest of the team leans in. He remains outcast, slouched in his chair, arms folded across his chest. Charlie suggests they move forward without him. Mofty agrees and offers this: "I've never made easier money."

"So, now, team. I know you've engaged yourselves after all. Sans Hall. So what? Let's throw some suggestive answers out on the table, shall we?

Name the one area of this planet we have not harvested raw energy?"

After another five minutes of thought, Cooper loudly says, "The ocean floor!"

The team nods and smiles as if they all passed some kind of test. They look up at Mack for approval.

Mack holds up the piece of paper in front of him. In large bold font, it reads:

DEEP SEA - OCEAN FLOOR.

"I believe we have a team consensus!" Mack smiles as the room erupts with applause. His teammates shake his hand, and Cooper slaps

him on the back.

"Nicely done, King." Hall says as he leaves the room, head bowed.

Mack is set to meet Kahtani at nine in the team conference room. The rest of the team is scheduled to meet at nine-thirty for the daily status readout. Mack arrives first a little early, true to form. He stands when the project manager enters the room and, in the midst of a firm, lengthy, and steady handshake accepts congratulations. Now Mack is told the team can at once move forward with a specific plan and that he is named team lead. So he agrees to sit in on Kahtani's upcoming afternoon meetings.

"Good morning, all." Kahtani welcomes the

team. "We have coffee, tea, bagels, fruit, and pastries. Please help yourselves. I'll be right back."

The team lunges into breakfast and chats noisily about sports, movies, music, current events. The seasoned pros don't waste time on politics or religion, nor anything work-related. Charlie and Mofty talk football. Kahtani returns with a folder in hand.

"Congratulations, team, on your breakthrough realization!"

They look at each other and then smile as they silently feel appreciation for Mack not having taken sole credit.

"I think we can all agree," Charlie says. "We could not have done it quite as it is without King."

"Well, thank you, Charlie. That's very nice," Mack adds. "But it was a team effort."

"Okay," Kahtani begins. "I've booked this room for the entire afternoon. Each of you will find an hour-long meeting proposal on your calendar. I'd like to spend an hour with each of you separately." And then for good measure, "Mack will you please plan on joining me for the afternoon?"

"Absolutely, sir."

Kahtani is not expecting anything new just yet bust asks anyway, "Any new status, team?"

"Regardless of what I'm about to share with you, sir, the team members should continue on with their analysis based on the simple notion that we will work deep on some ocean floor. That is enough for them to go on no matter what follows," Mack says.

"Duly noted, King. Go ahead."

"Okay then. My research shows, first, whether we target the deepest regions of the Atlantic Ocean or the Pacific Ocean. We can plan on working from as deep as six to eight miles. From there, our probes will go another three to six miles deeper through the rock. And I have already identified the shallowest and the deepest regions of both bodies of water."

"Doable, eh, Mr. King?"

"In my professional opinion, I'd say yes, certainly," Mack replies. "But we'll want to hear from the team too, you know."

"Of course. Still quite impressive, right?"

"It is indeed, Kahtani. But it is actually much shallower than I would've guessed before conducting this research."

"Indeed?"

"Yes, sir. But listen to this," Mack

continues, "secondly, and I bring this up not even as a remote possibility—not to be acted upon—research suggests evidence for potentially oceans worth of magma deep beneath the United States."

"What? What?" Kahtani gasps, astounded. "Oh my God, King! This is incredible! Is this true? Really?"

"Yes. And it seems quite more than just apparent, sir. Yet I reiterate, strongly, that we disregard the second point made indefinitely. I cannot stress this anymore firmly, resolutely, and solidly! Sir."

"All right, King. You take it and keep it in a safe place. As far as we are concerned, the team, me, you, we have no idea. This conversation never happened. You good?"

"Perfect, sir. I refuse to take it any further. It's not an option. Leave it to me."

"Okay, Mr. King." Kahtani gets to the business at hand for the afternoon. "Your role is expanded beyond your specialized and focused science. I'd like you to officially take on team leadership and act as technical, logical, physical, and application design consultant. Architect, good fit?"

"Leave anything out?" Mack laughs. "All right. Yes, sir." He welcomes the challenge. "That suits me well, and I believe I am well-suited for the tasks."

"Excellent, Mr. King. Thank you." Kahtani smiles and nods.

"Mr. Hall, please come in.

We would like you to narrow your area of concentration to 'probe and drill' as it relates to ocean floor discovery and harvest," Kahtani says.

"That is exactly what I've been thinking about, guys."

"Anything else?"

"No, sir. It's definitely perfect for me considering my area of expertise. And I'll have an apprentice or two on their way soon."

"Please have a seat, Charlie." Kahtani and Mack stand up and give her a big smile.

"Thank you."

"Charlie, we are working on zeroing in on your role, considering your area of expertise."

"Okay. Yes, this is good."

"We are thinking 'large-scale robotics' as it applies to underwater and ocean floor electronic, motor, and remote operations," Mack says.

"I am quite comfortable with that, and it makes total sense to me, considering our last team brainstorm and with the upcoming juniors."

"Very well, then, Charlie. Take it and run with it!" Kahtani says with a grin.

"Thank you, sirs."

"Come in and sit down, please, Mr. El Mofty."

"What is this all about?" Mofty asks.

"Probably nothing you are not already thinking about, sir, but just to cover our bases." Kahtani begins.

"Yes, okay."

"Let's get a more practical, detailed role description for you. Do you think you can do that for us?"

"Oh. Very good. Well…" Mofty begins.

"Yes? Please go on," Kahtani says.

"I see my role as both a taker and a giver. I take in the estimated and requested budget numbers from the collective teammates, respective to their area or task, etcetera, and I report out line item and total budget forecasts and actuals. I might guess that is within my realm to issue monetary-based warnings and to request funds from the project treasury, which I also oversee."

"Well, Mofty," Mack says. "You've been thinking about this, haven't you? Excellent job!"

"Mr. El Mofty, you have it right on, sir. Here it is all written out for you." Kahtani is pleased.

"Mr. Cooper, please come in!" Kahtani gives Cooper a big smile.

"Thanks for coming, Mr. Cooper," Mack says.

"So what's going on?" Cooper seems quite aloof and suspicious at the same time.

"We'd like to document your role in the project with more detail than 'mobilization,'" Kahtani says. "Have you given it any thought, particularly since the team brainstorm?"

"Some, yes."

"Well, let's see how this fits in with your own thoughts," Kahtani firmly says."You will lead on design and implementation of all mobile-related areas within the scope of this project. This means on water, underwater, and ocean floor mobilization. All things considered within the realm of this project."

"Including the…uh…classification, I take it?"

"Yes. Absolutely, Cooper," Mack answers.

"Much along the same lines, I've thought about the past couple days…nights." Cooper relaxes and grins at Mack and the project manager.

Mack reviews his team leader job requirements. The first task is to produce a system design diagram and narrative. The document heads and introduces all system-related and technical design and application deliverables. It remains a live document, a work in progress until all other subsystem designs are complete. It is the most visible document in the project portfolio.

The required style takes finesse, etiquette, and delivery know-how. He ties together all the subsystems into a manageable package, including a system design diagram that is easy to understand and narrative written in that hybrid technical writing technique he does so well, which appropriately reaches both the target business and technical audiences.

Mack doesn't recognize the CAD software—it's not a name brand—but all CAD packages behave pretty much the same. This one is just as pretty, sexy, and slick as any he has used. He builds three prototype mock-ups to keep a placeholder in his project workbook until Hall, Charlie, and Cooper produce their own design. He uses his figures as the source stock input to his overall system-design document.

The high-level, object-oriented design document identifies actors as scientists. The location is loosely defined as the deepest part of the Atlantic Ocean. The action equates to a mission, and the operators a high tech, deep-sea ship and submarine pair. He even uses thought bubbles. The atomic task is to implant tailored hypothermal shock-measuring probes into the ocean floor.

Kahtani looks over the project calendar and reviews project status reports as he chooses the words to speak for the coming directive from him to the other members. He is on time and under budget, his project manager priorities seem over and above the project mechanics themselves.

"Knock, knock," Mack says, standing at the doorway. He can see Kahtani is nose down into one document or another.

"Oh." He looks up. "King, come in and take a seat. I managed to reserve this room for an all-day team session."

"Excellent, sir," Mack says. "So we're here to issue the nudge from physical modeling to detail and development?"

"That's right, King, but I also have a question, a request of sorts for you."

"Shoot."

"I think you are the best person for this job: lead recruitment and hiring alongside your counterparts. What do you think? I know this may be a surprise to you."

"Actually, Kahtani," Mack words his response, "I've lately wondered how and who might handle that and have done some thinking about it. So it is not a total surprise. It's not something I can't handle, and I believe I may have a resource pool at the ready. In fact, the Interviewing process was something I did day after day for quite a while—scripts and questions, debriefing, the whole bit."

"You've approached them?"

"No, sir, no. Not yet. But I am prepared to. We'll work together. Respect, you know?"

"I am sincerely pleased with your forethought. You're a valuable partner, my friend."

"Well, thank you. Seems like second nature to me."

"Okay," Kahtani concludes, "let's suspend our conversation until the team arrives. Still thirty minutes away."

"I'm going to go back to my office and dig a little more into my recruitment ideas and notes. See you in thirty."

The individual team leaders arrive one by one, all more or less on time. These notices and actions, and all other personal-type-and-driven exercises are completely esoteric. Kahtani always has his eye on what truly matters, and that would be strictly project-related habits and work ethic. He knows he has an expert and dedicated team and an exceptional lead in King.

"Welcome, everybody!" Kahtani begins. "To this point, I am happy to confirm we are right on target in every management sense and aspect."

The team applauds.

"As outlined, today, with all the approvals and cross-reference approvals signed off-on, we are going to talk about next steps. First, I will ask King to talk to us about recruitment and team building. Afterward, we will introduce and validate our respective deliverables. Sound good?"

Everyone nods and assertively comments.

"Excellent! King, please take the floor and talk to the hiring logistics."

"Everyone," Mack starts off, "I have a pool of human resources, all of varying talent, skill sets, and specialty. The tank is virtually bottomless, and having worked with this private institution extensively in the past, I think we may even be able to bring in everyone we need within the young professional candidates from this particular pool of resources."

Mack goes on to explain how the consultancy at the institute essentially works. The candidates are cream of the crop recent graduates. They aim to work hard, follow direction, and behave well beyond their years in the field. He has everyone convinced and extremely pleased. None of them have the experience or interest Mack has in scripting interviews, facilitating them or conducting a post-interview review. Having worked extensively in support of HR—human resources—he has the entire arc of the hiring process well under management and discipline.

"I would like to collect the job titles, job descriptions, and resource requirements for each position you need. I hope two weeks is enough time for you to prepare and package these and the other HR-related items."

Mack says he will coordinate with the institute and arrange interviews. These will be held outside the absolute work environment in a conference room just down the hall from the secured entrance. He estimates the interviews will begin within two weeks.

"Let's break for lunch, King," Kahtani breaks in. "Okay?"

"Of course. It feels a bit overdue." Mack laughs. Everyone leans back and takes a breath. They are indeed ready for lunch. Joan leads the caterers into the room. Once again, she and Kahtani have outdone themselves with the menu and fare today. They all dig in, quietly enjoying the gourmet food.

Mack spends the first hour of the afternoon talking through an accelerated HR boot camp for his partners. He hands out guideline binders full of the processes involved. They are asked to pay attention to what he has to say and to look through and study the material afterward. They have to at least *look* like they know what they 're doing!

"Thank you, King," Kahtani offers. "Now let's go around the table and confirm the output of your designs to this point and what comes next. This obviously suggests a commingling with the job requirements for which you'll be using to build out your respective teams."

Mack begins his leg of the discussion first. Science of and physical, detailed creation of ballistic trajectory and detonation, and the system technology behind those tasks. His team will build out the probe insertions as well. He intends to sign a private hardware servicing contractor for all the hardware elements necessary.

Kahtani expects similar readouts from the others.

"Joan will continue floor management at Sleepy Hollow labs but will take on additional roles of special executive administrator, supporting King and myself on your behalf."

Hall discloses his drilling team will be set to go by the time they are assembled. Team throughput includes science of and physical, detailed creation in that capacity, and the system technology behind those tasks. His team will build out the underwater and horizontal-enabled drilling as well.

"I should suggest right here," Mack says, "that we all use the same contractor I have lined up for the hardware essentials of your tasks."

"Yes, please," Kahtani seconds it. "Let's please do that."

Charlie speaks up in her affecting singsong French accent.

"I am certain that I will need twice the amount of junior teammates than the rest of you and that I have been instructed to consider. Six developers are just not sufficient for the tasks we will have produced in the end. May I suggest bringing on twelve, King? Kahtani?"

Considering robotics and engineering scope, branches of mechanical and electrical engineering, plus computer science, the request is clearly fair. She requests understanding from the others and asks Mack and Kahtani give her their blessing. It makes sense that robotics, especially in this amplitude and reach, deserve the support she asks for. And so she gets what she needs.

"Mofty," Kahtani calls out. "Talk to us about budget status, out view, and any comments and concerns you may have."

"All is well and good. As I reported to you, we are on time and under budget. I expect another round of funding contributions within ninety days."

"Excellent, Mofty! Thank you." Kahtani is all smiles.

Cooper explains the inherent need for his team to couple and work with all the other teams. They all require automotive solutions at the ready.

——— ❧ **10** ❧ ———

It gets easier with every report submitted for Mack to build justification behind the project he agreed to escort to fruition. Solar and wind energy account for a trivial proportion of current renewables—about one-third of one percentage point. The vast majority still comes from biomass or wood and plant material—humanity's oldest energy source. While biomass is renewable, he learns, it is often neither good nor sustainable.

Burning wood in preindustrial Western Europe caused massive deforestation as is occurring in much of the developing world today. The indoor air pollution that biomass produces kills more than three million people annually. Likewise, modern energy crops increase deforestation, displace agriculture, and push up food prices. Despite the facts, Mack is quite aware of, and sympathizes with, activist groups crying out for the biomass solution.

Upon reading Mack's introductory reports, the team is shocked to learn that the most renewables-intensive places in the world are also the poorest. Africa gets almost 50 percent of its energy from renewables, compared to just 8 percent for the Organization for Economic Cooperation and Development. Even the European OECD countries, at 11 percent, are below the global average. Mack incorporates these findings in the "Appendix" section of his technical project statement.

While he insists within self that the

clean energy solution comes with renewables, the odd reality is that humanity has spent recent centuries getting away from renewables. Mack shakes his head but must give in to the rudimental fact that in 1800, the world obtained 94 percent of its energy from renewable sources. That figure has been declining ever since—a simple quirky truth of the matter.

Whether he wants to believe it or not, the momentous move toward fossil fuels has done a lot of good. Compared to 250 years ago, the average person in the United Kingdom today has access to 50 times more power, travels 250 times farther, and has 37,500 times more light. Incomes have increased twentyfold.

The switch to fossil fuels, contrary to skewed rumor, has also delivered some tremendous environmental benefits. Kerosene saved the whales, which had been hunted almost to extinction to provide supposedly "renewable" whale oil for lighting. Coal saved Europe's forests. With electrification, indoor air pollution, which is much more dangerous than outdoor air pollution, disappeared in most of the developed world. Mack transposes his thoughts:

*Realizing these facts, right here—right now—makes challenging the project seem shortsighted, senseless, even. And there is one environmental benefit that is often overlooked: in 1910, more than 30 percent of farmland in the United States was used to produce fodder for horses and mules. Tractors and cars eradicated this huge demand on farmland while ridding cities of manure pollution. Of course, fossil fuels bring their own environmental problems.*While technological innovations like scrubbers on smokestacks and catalytic converters on cars have reduced local air pollution substantially, the problem of carbon dioxide emissions remain. Mack sees and hears about it every day, even more so while performing the analysis for the project—that is the main reason for the world's clamor today for a return to renewables.

Mack creates a new worksheet with which he extrapolates some raw data regarding solar and wind power. In the most optimistic scenario, which assumes that the world's governments will fulfill all of their green promises, wind will provide 1.3 percent of global energy by 2035, while solar will provide 0.4 percent. Global renewables will most likely increase by roughly 1.5 percentage points to 14.5 percent by 2035. Under unrealistically optimistic assumptions, the share could increase five percentage points to 7.9 percent.

Therefore, solar and wind will contribute, but contribute little in the coming decades.

In the United States, renewables account for 9 percent of energy production in 1949. That number, almost a century later, may increase slightly, to 10.8 percent by 2040. In China, renewables' share in energy production dropped from 40 percent in 1971 to 11 percent today in 2029, and in 2035, it will likely be just 9 percent. Additionally, renewables are no less expensive today than any time in the past.

So current green energy policies are failing for a simple reason: renewables are far too expensive. Sometimes people claim that renewables are actually cheaper. But if renewables were cheaper, they wouldn't need subsidies, and we wouldn't need idiotic climate policies.

And the solution is to innovate the price of renewables downward. We need a dramatic increase in funding for research and development to make the next generations of wind, solar, and biomass energy cheaper and more effective.

When green renewables are cheaper than fossil fuels, they will take over the world. Instead of believing in the fantasies put forth by ill-advised activists, we should start investing in true green research and development based on realism and fact.

In some strange pseudoirony and reasoning, the International Energy Commission and the Global Warming Federation, of all groups, are the documented sponsors of the International Energy Commission's advanced energy project. It is unscrupulous, Mack easily recognizes, that these agencies and leagues would rather overwhelm the public with dirt-cheap legacy energy than admit, albeit over three decades, they still cannot deliver on their promises of renewable energy. And thus, they set forth work to bring the cost of renewables down.

The Department of Energy, Office of Scientific and Technical Information, and the US Department of Commerce, National Technical Information Service, are the project stakeholders. These factions are led by the United States; however, the project is also financed by individual, singleton world monetary powers and also by countries such as Nigeria, Ghana, Uganda, Tanzania, and Mozambique that remain poor even though they are resource rich.

According to Mack's analysis, on average, resource-rich countries have done even more poorly than countries without resources. They have grown more slowly and with greater inequality—just the opposite of what he would expect. After all, taxing natural resources at high rates will not cause them to disappear, which means that countries whose major source of revenue is natural resources can use them to finance education, health care, development, and redistribution. Mack spends the rest of the week studying the queer phenomenon:

Three of the curse's economic ingredients are well known: resource-rich countries tend to have strong currencies, which impede other exports; resource extraction often entails little job creation, thus unemployment rises; volatile resource prices cause growth to be unstable, aided by international banks that rush in when commodity prices are high and rush out in the downturns—reflecting the time-honored principle that bankers lend only to those who do not need their money.

Moreover, resource-rich countries often do not pursue sustainable growth strategies.

They fail to recognize that if they do not reinvest their resource wealth into productive investments above ground, they are actually becoming poorer. Political dysfunction exacerbates the problem as conflict over access to resource rents gives rise to corrupt and undemocratic governments.

Mack believes antidotes must exist to the problems; after all, resources should be a blessing, not a curse. Certainly, they can be! But it will not happen on its own, and it will not happen easily. It seems oil can indeed be a curse. Natural gas, copper, and diamonds, Mack notes, are also bad for a country's health. One way or another, oil—or gold or zinc—seems to make you poor. This fact is hard to swallow, and Mack is quick to note the exceptions such as Norway and the United States, which are often used to argue that oil and prosperity for all can indeed come together.

Delving further into the subject, he concludes the rarity of such exceptions confirms the rule. But his analysis also shows what it takes to avoid the misery-inducing consequences of wealth based on natural resources: democracy, transparency, and effective public institutions that are responsive to citizens.

These are important preconditions for more technical aspects of the recipe, including the need to maintain macroeconomic stability, manage public finances prudently, invest part of the windfall abroad, set up "rainy-day funds," diversify the economy, and ensure the local currency does not reach too high a price.

It all sounds sensible, but unfortunately, for most underdeveloped countries, these suggested defenses are as utopian as the larger goal they are supposed to help achieve. Countries that already have all these institutional strengths need not worry about the resource curse. For the rest, like an autoimmune disease, the curse undermines the ability of a country to build defenses against it. Concentrated power, corruption, and the ability of governments to ignore the needs of their populations make the curse hard to resist.

All may, but do not necessarily, add positively to the argument for renewable energy.

Mack files the arguments in his growing Renewable Energy folder: a hidden password-protected directory. The hard copy stays in the backflap of his personal portfolio.

Even under his in-depth research and discovery, Mack is not able to confirm the notion that the world's oil supply, notably reserves, is in dire straits. Oil reserves are the amount of technically and economically recoverable oil. Reserves may be for a well, for a reservoir, for a field, for a nation, or for the world. Different classifications of reserves are related to their degree of certainty.

The total estimated amount of oil in an oil reservoir, including both producible and nonproducible oil, is called "oil in place." However, because of reservoir characteristics and limitations in petroleum extraction technologies, only a fraction of this oil can be brought to the surface, and it is only this producible fraction that is considered to be reserves. The ratio of reserves to the total amount of oil in a particular reservoir is called the recovery factor. Determining a recovery factor for a given field depends on several features of the operation, including the method of oil recovery used and technological developments employed.

And because the geology of the subsurface cannot be examined directly, indirect techniques must be used to estimate the size and recoverability of the resource. Many oil-producing nations do not reveal their reservoir-engineering field data and instead provide unaudited claims for their oil reserves. The numbers disclosed by some national governments are suspected of being manipulated for political reasons.

Therefore, oil reserves may be higher or lower than what is reported. But we will disclose. I will find a way.

And meanwhile, OPEC continues their "fact"-finding mission.

II
CRACKING THE NADIR

The argosy moors in a slip of alcove that could not be any calmer or blue. The crew sleeps later than usual after an anchoring celebration the night before. These ships originally were typically large trading vessels in the seventeenth century. The argosy has a substantial cargo capacity, which in turn makes it difficult to maneuver and control in foul weather. No existing examples of these ships have ever been excavated or otherwise recovered, though Skip remodeled his beautifully and safely.

"Collin." Skip rousts everybody up for the

day. "Come on up, mate. After breakfast, I've got plans for us."

The converted pirate ship makes room for twelve plus up to a six-man crew. On this cruise, First Mate Collin and his wife, Kerry, accompany and join Skipper and his girlfriend Jill. They are three days away from the pirate ship party they threw between and in the middle of St. Thomas, St. Croix, St. John, Tortola, and Virgin Gorda with nudity, open sex, body shots, and shouts of boisterous fun—lively and pleasant— and merriment entertainment. It is no wonder Skip's small crew remains in exhausted solace.

"I don't know where you get it from," Collin says to Skip. "I suppose you were just born to take it all on!" They both laugh.

"Well, Mate, I suppose we are here at our destination. Take a look."

"Rockall?" Collin asks incredibly. "Seriously, already?"

"That's right," Skip says to Collin. "It looks so much larger than the photos we've been looking over, eh?"

"And look at the glimmer. How bright it looks in the sunlight!"

"We'll paddle over after we eat," Skip says.

Conversations over a hearty early meal revolve around all the chit and transcripts Skip picked up here and there on the way to the foreordination."Rockall is an uninhabited remote granite islet of the United Kingdom in the North Atlantic Ocean situated," Skipper leads off, skimming the article. "It's situated at a rough distance from the closest large islands: Northwest of Ireland, West of Great Britain, and South of Iceland."

"I thought it was within the United Kingdom's exclusive economic zone," Collin asserts, "and in 1973 became part of the Na h-Eileanan Siar council area, which comprises the Outer Hebrides."

"Ah, Collin, it is, however, designated as belonging to *no* specific electoral ward at all! Ha! Fancy that."

The nearest permanently inhabited place is North Uist, an island in the Outer Hebrides of Scotland, 230 miles to the east.

"Oh, I can't wait to get there!" Kerry exclaims.

"I say we do it naked!" Jill answers. Everyone laughs.

"No, really. Let's come on, please?"

So they wear their swimwear over in the dingy and plan to strip once on land. As they begin the short trip over to Rockall, Kerry asks, "Where does the name 'Skip's Swill' come from?"

"Thirty years ago I owned a beach bar on Clearwater Beach, Florida, called Skip's. At the end of every night, all the bottles left with below two ounces or so were poured into a common bottle."

"Are you serious?" Collin hadn't heard anything about this before.

"Quicker than you might have imagined, the bottles filled fast. We labeled them "Skip's Swill."

"Well, what did you do with them?" Jill asks.

"It got to the point of three full walls of shelves in my office housed the fifths of Swill."

"Yeah?" Collin goads. "Then what?"

"Well," Skip begins, "whenever a band came in that kicked ass—exceptional rock shows—a cut above the rest, I awarded them a sacred bottle of Skip's Swill. You know you're good if you get a bottle of Swill!"

"Oh my god, that's crazy!" Kerry screeches. "What did that shit taste like?"

"To be fair," Skip answers, "it varied, but each bottle tasted kind of like a cross between a Zombie and a Long Island Iced Tea."

"Wow," Jill replies. "That is so cool!"

"Truth be told," boasts Skip, "it became a well-known complimentary gift for a job well-done. Sort of an accolade or trophy."

"Wow." Collin sighs.

"Yeah, folks," Skip speaks to all. "Skip's Swill brings back what those were some fine days, indeed."

"Okay!" Kerry announces. "We're here. Everybody strips!"

The men were drawn to a large peak of a rock. It indicates since the late-sixteenth century, the sixty-foot rock has been noted in written records.

"Although I submit," Skip says, "it is likely that some northern Atlantic fishermen knew of the rock before these historical accounts were made. I read that in the twentieth century, the location of the islet became a major interest due to the potential oil and fishing rights, spurring continued debate amongst several European nations."

"It's just a rock," Collin says.

"Read this one," Skip says.

Collin reads aloud: "Lord Kennet said of it in 1971, 'There can be no place more desolate, despairing, and awful.' It gives its name to one of the sea areas named in the shipping forecast provided by the British Meteorological Office."

"Jesus." The two girls scoff in unison.

"Let me read this to you, Collin. For what a so-called wasteland, this is dubbed. Rockall has been a point of interest for adventurers and amateur radio operators who have variously landed on or briefly occupied the islet. Fewer than twenty individuals have ever been confirmed to have landed on Rockall, and the longest continuous stay by an individual is currently forty-five days. And this is funny, listen. In a House of Commons debate in 1971, William Ross, MP for Kilmarnock said, 'More people have landed on the moon than have landed on Rockall.'"

"Let me see that thing." Collin grabs the log. "In 1956, the British scientist James Fisher referred to the island as 'the most isolated small rock in the oceans of the world.' The neighboring Hasselwood Rock and several other pinnacles of the surrounding Helen's Reef are smaller, at half the size of Rockall or less, and equally remote, but those formations are legally not islands or points on land, as they are often submerged completely, only revealed momentarily above certain types of ocean surface waves."

He reads on. "The United Kingdom claimed Rockall in 1955 and had previously claimed an extended exclusive economic zone based on it. This claim to an extended zone was dropped upon ratifying UNCLOS in 1997 since rocks or islets such as Rockall, which cannot sustain human habitation or economic life, are not entitled to an exclusive economic zone under the convention. However, such features are entitled to a territorial sea extending twelve nautical miles. The UK's claim to territorial waters around Rockall was previously disputed by Ireland on the basis of uncertain ownership of the rock. With effect from 31 March 2014, the UK and Ireland published EEZ limits, which resolved any disputes over the ownership of the islet. I mean holy shit!"

"Aw, come on Collin, Jesus Christ, enough already." Kerry wants to explore.

"No…wait. Just a little bit more to go.

In response to a Freedom of Information Act request, the British government has said, 'The islet of Rockall is part of the UK: specifically, it forms part of Scotland under the Island of Rockall Act 1972. No other state has disputed our claim to the islet.'"

"Guys, guys," Jill calls out to the men. "We found a path going around by this small bay!"

"The cacti look amazing," Kerry says. "Oh look! Look! Two iguanas playing, running after each other up and down the tree!"

"Aww." Jill is amazed and starts to giggle.

Just as the group begins to wonder where the path goes, they stop, frozen and enchanted.

"Oh my

God!" Kerry exclaims.

The path led them to a beachfront. It is completely covered in bright shiny white coral. Some obviously washed ashore and left, but there are setups and vignettes formed of coral pieces and driftwood. Many are exotic, erotic, and even neurotic. They followed each other around the entire area marveled at the sight. Some figurines have a cross between the coral, driftwood, and rags.

"Let's make something. Let's each make one

of our own. Anything goes! Come on!" Jill says excitedly.

Along the ground and among the rocks and with the driftwood, the group goes to work. Kerry finds the coral to make a couple hand in hand, the woman with colossal breasts and a man with a penis longer than this legs.

Collin finds a piece of fabric. He forms a pair of old farmers out of coral with a shovel and pitchfork out of driftwood.

Jill out-sexed Kerry easily by simulating a woman straddling a man's face. "Well hey!" she hollers back at Kerry. "You said anything goes."

Skip formed a vignette with two sexy nudes at a table eating a meal together.

Everyone examines each other's work, have a laugh and agree they have found a virtual resort just heavenly. But they also know sex on the ship is on the way. On the way back, they take a dip and then just carry their clothes into the dingy with them.

There is nothing better than afternoon, after sun, after swim, and after bizarre experiences than a nice tepidly cool shower. Except what will have come afterward. Both couples are locked into each other, engaged. They play calm, mellow, and comfortable. No doubt of satisfaction, both couples take a late after sex, afternoon nap.

Skip dreams of a storm knocking the boom or jib. It is bothersome but not so much to wake him. He hears it again. It will not stop. His eyes open and hears a knocking—it is at his cabin door."Hello?" he asks.

"Sorry, Skip." Collin sounds upset. "Skip?"

"Oh, Collin, it's you. Something wrong?"

"Did you hear that?"

"Hear what? I guess I didn't. I'll be right out. Jill is still sleeping."

"Okay, Collin, what is it?"

"I heard some kind of burst or detonation."

"What? Was it on the ship?"

"No, man, it sounded far away." Collin tries to explain. "It sounded muffled but incredibly powerful, forceful, potent."

"Just that one occurrence?"

"Yes. Just the one, Skip. It was enough to rouse and provoke me."

"And it was nowhere near the ship."

"No, Skip," Collin is shaken-up.

"Let's lie back down and try to get savory and soothe."

"Yes, sir."

There are no further cannonade or bursts

through the night. Still yet, however, anticipation keeps the two men awake. There's something funny going on here. Skips feels it. But what? Barometers and meters read odd, and the vessel takes on a gentle and hypnotic rocking with the increasing waves coming to it from the west.

They decide on a light breakfast, but Jill packs to take with them for lunch later on the small island. The foursome paddle to the shore. They decide to make it their quest to find that one piece of coral—he grail—that one specimen that draws them to lay claim and keep for a souvenir, like a talisman or peacekeeper, catalyst.

"Remember, everyone," Kerry begins. "The special piece will call you. It will beckon you. You'll know you have found it, or it's found you, it is as if God delivers it—the feeling—you will feel it!" She is so excitable and excited, it is contagious. All four of them are cracking up. Skip and Collin love their girls.

"Much wavier today than yesterday, huh?" Skip says.

"Sure is," Collin replies. "But I checked the forecast, and there are no storms near us."

They walk the narrow path past the small bay and within ten minutes, to the beach on the other side. It is not anymore a surprise after their discovery yesterday, but there resides the magic. Magic everywhere for every sense; in through the feet as they walk, the European sea salt. The magnificent historic sight, and the essence of ocean shore and water.

The small group stops on the way back at the alcove. Skipper announces he'll be snorkeling, and Jill says she'll go too.

Kerry spreads a large beach blanket. Collin stands up after smoothing a corner of the overspread.

"Ow! Ow!" Collin hurt himself. . Please look at the top center of my head."

"Oh Christ, Collin, you're bleeding."

"Jesus," Collin pleads as tough, starting a prayer. "Please relieve this pain. Ahhhhh. Jesus, please."

"Gonna go saturate this bandana with the salty sea. Hold on, Collin."

She kneels next to him and uses the compress. "Shit, my baby. Are you gonna be all right?"

"Oh, babe," Collin says. "I love you so much."

She reaches down with her other hand and plays with him. Before he knows it, she straddles him and takes him in. Nice and slow and warm, gliding up and grinding down. He tells her his headache feels better.

"You're so fine, Kerry."

As if on cue, they situate each other just as Skip and Jill trot up to the picnic spot. Skip and Jill heard all about head bump. Sitting around the blanket, preparing to eat, they spy a tall blonde woman twenty feet away strip down and lie down in her spot.

"Well now," Skip says and laughs. "Ain't this the place to be?"

Jill chuckles as she backslaps his upper arm. "Just don't stare, you perv!"

The group laughs as a picture-perfect picnic unfolds before them: juice, yogurt, and gourmet chicken salad sandwiches. Kerry even has for them a surprise pineapple upside-down cake! The food is validated unsurpassable by the silence on the blanket. Both couples lie down and nap, which takes them through the rest of the afternoon.

Collin lies unrestful in anticipation of the sound he heard the night before. Kerry lightly snores in her cute purring way, and eventually, as usual, lulls Collin to slumber. Skip is keen on the water. He's not thinking about possible noises, but he can feel his flotilla rocking ever slowly but significantly deeper.

Jill is up first, so she puts the coffee on and sits on a helm chair, sipping, and takes long soothing breath of salt air. The slow rocking motion of the big wooden ship on the water helps ease her into another awesome and fabulous day. What is not to love? The argosy? The travels to practically every sea on the sunny earth? Living like a pirate, but one with a white hat? Your lover? Your best friends in the whole world? Jill loves her life right now.

"Good mooooorning," Kerry sings out as she comes up on board from the steps to the cabins below. "Ohm, mmm, this coffee is so good."

"Enjoy!" Jill says.

"Another beautiful day is on the way," Kerry says. "Just look as this, Jill!"

"I'm just surprised to be up before the boys," Jill says. "I like to know they get the rest they deserve, though."

"Haven't these day trips to Rockall been fantastic?"

"Oh yeah, Kerry. So great." Jill laughs. "I can't believe how easy it was to get the men to do naked exploration. That, my friend, is sexy."

"Sure is."

"Oh, by the way, we saw you screwing under the tree." Jill giggles.

Kerry begins the head-bump story as Jill waves it away and tells her not to bother. Both girls laugh out loud. Chatter of where the day may take them comes up. Neither care, but they do agree they'd like to have another day moored right there where they're at.

"Mmm," Kerry whispers. "So good."

"Oh yah, sweetie." Jill sighs and adds, "I think the guys are planning some scuba diving today."

"Yes, they are or were talking about it yesterday." Kerry innocently scoffs.

"Hey, Kerry." Jill has a question for Kerry. "Look out at the horizon."

"Yeah?"

"Does it look as though there is a black line hovering at, or over, or resting upon the horizon?"

"A black line?" Kerry asks.

"Yes. Kind of. Between the water and the sky. Do you see it?"

"No, Jill, I don't see anything."

"Hmmm, okay. Now it seems gone."

Skip is in the galley rattling pots, pans, and utensils. Collin is up and trots up the ship's ladder stairs.

"Good morning, ladies!" Collin says with a big smile.

"Hey, you," Kerry says, pulling him in for a kiss.

"Morning, Collin," Jill says. "I hear Skip is taking on breakfast."

"You would be right, Jill. Not sure what exactly, but who messes up a breakfast?"

"So we shouldn't be frightened?" Jill laughs along with the group. Skip actually does quite well around a kitchen. Quite a good cook at sea, which means that the girls will have to take over KP—dishwashing duty—kitchen patrol. Not bad since they are actually used to having to do both!

The dinner bell rings and rousts everybody down to the eating table. Skip serves up shrimp and grits, thick-cut bacon and poached egg on English muffins. There is a bowl of fruit salad on the side for everyone to dip in to.

"This could not be a better breakfast, pal," Collin says.

"Great job, honey," Jill says and means it.

"It's wonderful, Skip."

"Thanks, Kerry. Thanks everybody. Enjoy!"

Jill asks, "Are you still planning to go scuba diving today?"

"I'm planning on it," Skip answers.

"With you on that, my man," Collin says with a big smile.

"You girls want to come for a dive?" Skip asks.

The two girls look at each other, shake their heads, and politely decline.

"I think we're going to do some sunbathing au naturel," Kerry says.

"Yeah, and you know," Jill adds. "Every twenty or thirty minutes take a quick dip."

"Well, we damn sure like the sound of

that, eh, Collin?" Skip is laughing at his own comedic sounding reply.

"Dive first," Collin says simply, "and all sorts of fun in the sun a little later!"

"Oh, yeah, okay, Collin," Kerry says. "All sorts of diving all over!"

Everyone is cracking up out loud as the girls begin to clean up the galley. The guys walk down a flight and gather their scuba gear there at the stern starboard corner of the Skip's Swill.

12

Not much chatter while the girls lie on the chaises. They flip from front to back every twenty minutes or so. Somehow, instinctively, they both rise at the same time to jump or step into the water. It is immaculate though cooler than the prior port down in St. John. But considering location, not bad, and holding so much heat from the sun, the cool ocean feels welcome.

Jill reels up the thermometer. The water is approaching seventy-one degrees. In midsummer, that is not bad at all and is refreshing.

"About seventy-one degrees, Kerry."

"Not bad for the Irish Seas," Kerry says. "We're not in the islands anymore! Maybe I'll feel more at home when we visit Dublin in a couple weeks." The young woman of Irish descent is excited to visit her ancestral country and drink some good ale.

"Oh, look," Jill says and points at the trailing bubbles.

Two hooded, masked heads bloop up from the water. They both discard from their mouths the oxygen intake valve piece.

"Ahoy, ladies!" Skip bellows.

"Where are you going to be, Skipper?" Jill asks.

"Our plan is to cover a track about fifty-feet wide from here—being center point—to Rockall. Give us ninety minutes or so. No longer."

"Okay, have fun and be careful!"

"Thanks, sweetie," Skip replies to Jill. "Love ya."

"Love you too!"

Skip has as much cold-water diving experience as warm-water experience. Warm-water diving is usually preferred for the unbelievably blue water and colorful coral reefs. They are indeed a sight to see. Not to mention all the colorful fish. The last few weeks in St. John were made priceless by the diving experience.

"So, Skip?" Collin asks. "I've never been cold-water diving. How bad is it?" he asks facetiously.

"What I like most about warm-water diving is that you do not need a hood and gloves like you do in cold water. When getting geared up for diving in cold water, putting on the hood is somewhat of a pain."

"Yeah. Okay. I get that."

"Once in the cold water, though, you'll be happy to have it on. A good trade for the sights to be seen. The same goes for the gloves. It takes some getting used to when reaching for the dive equipment with the gloves on, but you'll be glad to have them on midway through the dive."

As much as he likes warm-water diving, he fully admits he likes cold-water diving just as much. As soon as he gets his dry suit on, he knows his cold-water dives will be just as good as the warm-water ones.

"Plus, my friend, because you don't get wet in a dry suit! What a concept. Being able to be in water and not get wet." They both laugh aloud.

"Not many amateurs know this, when it comes to hypothermia, you need to be just as safe in warm water as you do in cold water. Depending on conditions and preference," Skip explains, "divers should wear at least a one-to-three millimeter wet suit when diving in warm water."

"Hypothermia in warm water?" Collin asks.

Skip grabs one of his dive manuals. "Here. Read the first couple paragraphs."

Collin reads in a whisper, "As stated in the NOAA Diving Manual: Divers also have to be wary of hypothermia in warm environments. A phenomenon called 'warm water hypothermia' can occur even in the tropics, especially during long dives and repetitive dives made without adequate rewarming between dives.

In warm-water hypothermia, long slow cooling can take place in water temperatures as warm as eighty-two degrees Fahrenheit to ninety-one degrees. Although warm-water hypothermia is not easily recognized as its cold water counterpart, it definitely warrants attention. Interesting. Wow."

"When I dive in cold water," Skips says, "I can tell when I'm ready to get out of the water. I start to shiver. Not so much in warm water. I didn't feel my body get cold during our dives the past couple weeks. We only did two dives a day for five days in St. John, for example, but if I would have done more than twice a day, I might have gotten cold in warm water."

"So, Skipper," Collin caps the conversation. "In conclusion, since experiencing both cold and warm water, your consensus is that you simply like both."

"You got it, Collin!" And into the Atlantic they go. Until they reach the halfway point to Rockall, Skip and Collin are diving deep.

After an evening meal, Kerry lies down next to Collin on their bunk. He finds a reference book about cold-water corals and reads."Corals are not just warm-water creatures. They also live at depths of 135 feet down to 6,562 feet, in water temperatures as low as 36 degrees Fahrenheit.

Although fishermen and scientists have known about cold-water corals for nearly 250 years, it's only in the past several years that the combination of advanced technology and political will began to explore them.

Unlike tropical corals, cold-water corals don't have symbiotic algae living in their polyps so they don't need sunlight to survive. They feed solely by capturing food particles from the surrounding water. Their polyps tend to be much bigger than tropical corals. Therefore, they are very clearly visible and seen.

"Cold-water coral reefs are commonly found where current flow is accelerated. They are found on the continental shelf and also in deep-sea areas with topographic highs, such as seamounts, mounds, ridges, and pinnacles.

Deep-sea corals grow slowly, perhaps half an inch a year, but over time, they form extensive reefs. The largest reef yet discovered, off the coast of Norway's Røst Island, is 131,233 feet long and 9,842 feet wide. Another Norwegian reef has grown to a height of 542 feet above the surrounding seabed. Radiocarbon dating of coral from the Sula Ridge off Norway suggests that the reef complex, the second largest in the Northeast Atlantic Ocean, has been growing for around eight thousand years."Deep-sea coral reefs are made up of only a few coral species, but they provide a home for many other animals, including sea fans, sponges, worms, starfish, brittle stars, sea urchins, crustaceans, and fish.

The number of invertebrate species on reefs in the Northeast Atlantic Ocean can be as high as that found in shallow-water tropical reefs. Although the number of fish species is relatively low (twenty to forty species compared to three thousand species on some tropical reefs), cold-water coral reefs do attract large masses of fish and, like their tropical cousins, serve as important spawning and nursery grounds."

He reads Kerry to sleep long ago, and with that read, Collin involuntarily calls it a night. He is snoring in moments. Kerry is already sleeping, so that is no bother to her. Skip and Jill lie on chaises, side by side, holding hands and enjoy moonlight cocktails and chat on deck.

"It was curiously murky down there today," Skip says to Jill. "Collin wouldn't have noticed, of course, since he's never dived deep before."

"Does that worry you?" Jill asks.

"Well, no. It's not a worry. It's more of an annoying thought provoker."

"Let me tell you what I saw earlier," Jill says to Skipper.

"As I gazed across the horizon, there appeared to be a dark black line right there at the edge of that place right between the surface area, you know, the water and the sky."

"Really?"

"Yes, Skip. It looked like a horizontal straight line of jet black magic marker or paint stroke."

"Let me think. That's odd at the outset, but just wait."

"Okay."

"I hate to say this, Jill," Skip says. "But we may want to consider continuing on sometime sooner than planned, like within a few days."

"Is there something wrong?"

"No. But we might have some kind of little storm coming this way."

"Oh."

"I would just hate to ruin a good time. You know. Leave at a high point!"

They both chuckle and clink glasses.

"Cheers."

"Cheers."

$$\text{---}\ \text{13}\ \text{---}$$

Skip wakes to the feel that the Swill is being pulled or pushed toward Rockall or in that direction. At the least, that is his immediate sense. He hurries up to the deck. The ship is rocking both stern to bow and starboard to port. He holds on to a foremast to steady himself.

The wind blows hard. His hair flies back, and his baggy shorts ruffle from front to back, like he is standing behind an everglades fan boat. He goes to the steering station to check some stats. The wind is at Beaufort

Scale 7; high wind, overmoderate gale, and near gale force.

On his way back down to the deck, he is knocked off the ladder by the wind; his head slams onto the deck, and he goes out cold and bleeding from the skull. Jill reaches the deck just in time to witness the assault and runs to tend to him, oblivious of the conditions.

Collin and Kerry reach the deck together. They look west just in time to see a whale tail slapping. Tail slapping is something that is seen a lot. It does not appear to be an aggressive expression. When two whales are tail slapping at the same time, it seems that they are trying to outperform one another.

Tail slapping can be heard underwater by other whales many miles away, so it may also be a method of letting other whales know they are in the area in the case of single whale's tail slapping. Tail slapping would also be helpful in removing a buildup of barnacles from the tail. The force of the tail hitting the water over time would certainly assist in removing parasites and barnacles.

But the three helpless souls on ship look up as the whale's tail slams against the ship as it plummets and plunges, disappearing into the water. They scream as beyond they see it—a wall of sea easily a dozen times the size of an Imax movie screen. It is moving into them like a wave but holds the form of a wall.

Collin and Kerry make it to Jill and they all huddle and hug. Everyone is soaking wet, screaming and crying. The argosy belongs to the tsunami now. The vessel is broken away and apart as it rolls over twice and slams into Rockall Island. The wall of water breaks up as it rushes over the island, the ship and the smaller land mass beyond.

Swill sits atop the pinnacle point of stone that tops Rockall. It is upside down as the highest point of Rockall protrudes through the upside-down bottom of the once gorgeous ship.

The tsunami hits and rolls on, broken up and slowed by contact into the eastern side neighbor islands to Rockall: Soay, St Kilda, Scotland.

News quickly spreads throughout the region, then the world about the unforeseen and forceful tsunami, with much discussion around the cause or source of it. It is too early to back search the oceanic area. Meteorologists, scientists, oceanographers, and seismologists are all struggling to discover the cause, the fault, and reason for it all. There were no alerts from anywhere. There exists no fault line or volcano anywhere near the location of impact or following the presumed trail behind it.

—◦✣ **14** ✣◦—

Kahtani's executive project summary reads, in part, and explains in simple terms the background information that borne and drives the project."Not all energy resources are accessible on land or in shallow water. Large oil deposits reside buried deep under the ocean floor.

Using equipment, we determine the probing, drilling, and detonation sites most likely to produce oil, gas, coal, and shale. We use a mobile submarine offshore drilling unit to dig into the initial mine or chasm. Our production units enable a switch from penetration to capture once the resource is found.

"Oil companies replace the mobile rigs with a more everlasting production apparatus. Our job is to drill down into the ocean's floor, open up the surrounding quarry to find deposits. The part of the drill that extends below the deck and through the water, the riser, allows for excavated substances to move between the floor and the rig. We use robotic engineers to lower a drill string—a series of pipes designed to drill down to the deposit—through the riser.

"Our manufactured 'Subsea Systems' are actually wellheads, which sit on the seafloor and extract resources straight from the field. We use pipes to force the find back up to the floor and siphon it to nearby platform rigs, a submarine overhead, a local production hub, with consideration to a more faraway even onshore site. This makes the Subsea System very versatile and the popular choice for us.

Types of systems discarded due to the project classification baseline include fixed platforms, jack-up rigs, compliant-tower rig, floating production system, tension-leg platform, and spar platform.

Please see Appendix A for a full definition and team lead output analysis of these aforementioned systems."

"We are currently conducting live-tests in the North Atlantic," Kahtani explains. "The probes go many miles deep and returns data illustrating the effects of coal, oil, shale, and gas mining on a global basis—meaning, we will reuse the probes and process at all target sites before actual processing is approved.

Let me introduce Dr. Hall. He and Dr. King designed our exclusive sensor, probes, and excavating systems."

Hall describes in a high-level, pseudotechnical language written by King, suited for his audience, the essential properties of his systems. Optical-fiber sensors constitute an indispensable tool in the effort, helping engineers to not only locate resources, but also get the most out of them.

Due to target proximities, finding energy resources is one of the toughest engineering challenges. Once a candidate field is found, resource extraction is next in the sequential process and an even bigger challenge.

Mack steps in to introduce briefly most of the components: downhole sensors; acoustic, electronic signature sensors, pressure transducer sensors, proximitor systems, vibration and thrust transmitters, seismic sensor systems, flexible silicon pressure; mud sensor pressure transmitter, and most sensitive and critical of all, the submersible-pressure transmitters, differential pressures sensors, flame trackers, high temperature and seismic sensor systems, and the subsea wellhead in total.

The head sponsor from the United States introduces an Arabian sponsor and financier.

"So tell us, please, Mr. Al Kahtani," the robed man begins. "Are we behind the small tsunami that hit recently off the Scotland coast?"

Kahtani clears his throat and looks over at Mack and says, "Yes, gentleman."

"Mr. King, please briefly explain."

"This was our first end-to-end live test. We got to the detonation phase, and it initiated a movement in an unknown, almost indefectible, fault there."

"Other than that, my dear guests, the entire process—the test—is viewed as 80 percent successful." Kahtani hopes to finish the conversation. "Let us now enjoy a fine meal and continue over lighter, unofficial conversation."

After the late-afternoon dinner, Kahtani offers a trial list of next steps to his project sponsors. He is relieved that they did not raise a higher concern over the Rockall disaster.

15

Mack, neck-deep reviewing the methodologies that are successful to date against those not so and those still yet to be tested, sits in full resolve. Though it takes nights of desperate prayer to get this far. He has the site hardware, and workers scoot away from live test area, which is now crawling with investigators and cross-government agencies. He directs the appliances and workers toward the Mid-Southern Atlantic.

Charlie's remote control of deep-sea apparatus is a smashing success. All but two of her design and development team members are dismissed. She commands the eight-man crew that operates the robotic devices.

Mofty continues to monitor finances and budget. The project sponsors and stakeholders are extremely pleased that the project remains ahead of the curves in all monetary aspects. They regard the Rockall episode a mere speed bump.

Cooper's mobilization mechanisms perform perfectly on point. His few human and many automated resources below water that commingled with Charlie's robotics are miraculously successful from the start. Under Cooper, those team's disciplined system tests prove to pay off.

Hall's penetration equipment performs as expected, but he and select members of his team lead Mack's charge of fault line potential and detection. King's cracking the nadir detonation works but cannot be initiated again until his seismic projection, probing, and measurements are improved.

Oceanography, or oceanology, and marine science absorb initial efforts of the special task force. It is the branch of earth science that studies a wide range of topics, including marine organisms and ecosystem dynamics; ocean currents, waves, and geophysical fluid dynamics; plate tectonics and the geology of the seafloor.

The team concentration lay in examining the geology of the seafloor. The other diverse topics reflect multiple disciplines that oceanographers blend to gain further knowledge of the world of ocean and understanding of its processes. But that information, although offered–the presentation is tabled– is perhaps for later use.

"International submarine cables," Mack begins his lecture, "play an important role of global communication backbone because they carry a variety of important services. Natural disasters such as earthquakes, undersea landslides happen frequently and often cause the interruption of submarine cables.

After finding the fault location of submarine cable, telecommunication carriers will redistribute routes according to restoration plans to guarantee services for customers. Monitoring of the cable electricity power equipment is widely used for fault detection and concluding the fault's location.

"Even though the investment cost of this method is high, we will put effort on it. I propose also a new fault location analysis model to infer the submarine cable fault section from the characteristics that submarine cables carry multiservice and multidomain network devices.

Since submarine cables are broken, they will cause a mass of leased line alarms and voice circuit alarms. We make the correlation analysis from routes and alarms of circuits in the collection of submarine cables to analyze the possible submarine fault sections.

"We shall also use the alarms from dry contacts of submarine cable physical equipment to analyze other possible submarine fault sections. After converging and intersecting these possible submarine cable fault sections, we can conclude the real submarine cable fault sections. Extensive experimentation suggests, currently the rate of this model, an accuracy as high as 83 percent."

He concludes, "Our initial efforts must and will include improvement of the methodology just described."

Political wings connected with the project apply pressure to the project sponsors. Due to class status, their influence cannot be ignored. They want throughput, and they want it now. Energy resources, apart from the existing, kept private, restricted, and confidential, is a prize coveted so strongly that disastrous results getting to that prize matter not—even loss of life.

"I am not prepared yet," Mack tells Kahtani, "to set sights on a particular target. I'm sorry."

"Mr. King." Kahtani looks Mack squarely in the eye. "This is an order."

"I do not take orders, Kahtani."

"I am sorry, King, but you must conform immediately."

"So you are giving me an order, or is it an ultimatum?"

"Yes. I am."

"Consider me a conscientious objector."

"Mr. King! Let me remind you of the population of brass above this project and your head and of their power, shrewdness, single-and-focused vision."

"We are not prepared. Period."

"I will dock your pay, King."

"I'll walk, Kahtani."

"You can't walk, King. That cannot and will not happen."

"That so?"

"Please do not make me lead you down the path of dark understanding that comes with your attempted escape from or dismissal of this enterprise at this point."

"So what? What do you want me to do?

Please, *tell* me, Kahtani!" Mack scoffs in disgust.

"You have twenty-eight days to resolve all open issues. Your deliverable is a sworn, signed statement of completion and positive test results."

"That's all you need, huh?"

"No. There is one more thing. By the end of that twenty-eight-day period, you will have led the team to the first of the next preferred targeted site. That, Mr. King, is it."

"I see."

"Yes. For now." Kahtani stands and walks away.

The next site is a success and is producing on average eighty-five thousand barrels of crude oil per day. Postproduction includes placement of the pseudopermanent submarine pump or extraction gear and the storage vessel, which is a bladder of sorts. The mechanics and method of product pickup is established. This can be done two ways. The pickup underwater cruiser may either swap a fresh, empty bladder for the full one or syphon the material from the giant bead.

The probing instruments lead the parade of unearthing appliances south. The probes signal upon a prime choice encounter and then the preproduction and production submachines are assembled. They are brought up to a constant ready state. All this is a repeatable process roaming southerly from site to site in the mid-Atlantic.

"I am very pleased," Kahtani says to

Mack. "I should say *we* are very pleased with your performance: the new probes, the mobile units, the pseudopermanent build-out, and of course, the extraction and retrieval processes."

"I'm glad your project is a success," Mack replies dryly.

"So, King, our differences are fully behind us now? Our project, eh?"

"Yes, sir. They are." Mack's response is automated.

"Very good then. Oh, wait, I did want to mention this to you."

"What's that, Kahtani?"

"You've been awarded a $250,000 bonus for your efforts, dedication, and merit."

The organizations and units succeed in inserting the probes at the next sequential stop for the venture. The advanced energy production enterprise is in full swing, and altogether, the dozen running sites contribute 1,020,000 barrels of oil a day.

—————❈ **16** ❈—————

Mack sits in his recliner with a drink and notebook on the end table. He thinks of all the current oil-producing countries and how this, the Advanced Energy project and its sponsors, could possibly pull them together in a world of peace. Even through intended destruction, only to be rectified by the people who are blamed by world activists in the first place, will not foster accord and reconciliation. His thoughts jump to the deals that will have been made worldwide, and who wins and who loses.

Concept and premise are understandable,

okay, because along with good old oil drilling mechanics, the people merely put their minds on the marriage between that and the concept of submarine methodologies. Those basic general thoughts can be authored very believable. It is far enough away to keep the populations secure but initially and nervously guessing; thus, interested at the same time.

The mere high-level idea could easily and deservedly be a delivered story easily understood, but to delve into the possibilities and realities of the activities, though novel, are stand-alone *epic*.

It must be told…

The politicians and world leaders will do what they do for the sake of monetary gain that is fortunes. No one knows the *who*, *what*, *where*, and *how* of the increasingly available fuel; nor do people question the falling prices of it. Mack is sure, certain, that at some point, a statement will have to be issued, and some form of reason and resolution, at the very least, will have to be stated. The secrecy of the initiative cannot last forever.

The darkness fills Mack's thoughts riding along the twilight as it rises outside. He goes to bed every night and wakes every morning immersed in empathetic thought. His mind is suspended over the Rockall disaster, and what more could happen as the Advanced Energy initiative propels further, pinpricking the targeted, vulnerable sites.

Mack finishes his daily journal and adds to his personal project notebook. The nightly actions are a catalyst to sleep as he closes the notebook and turns off the nightstand lamp. His mind is clear and his conscience clean because he is on top.

He's not fearful of Kahtani, and he is unafraid of all involved in the project or with the operation. He is elevated within the core team to operations managing director. It's white glove: he no longer has to get his hands dirty. All the original project design team are middle managers over their operation's personnel, and all fall under Mack. And more and more money keeps on flowing in.

He takes responsibility for the Rockall incident, resolves the root cause issues, and turns the operation back into a successful endeavor. He is the operations go-to guy and point contact from top-down and bottom-up.

He spends his time extracting all the pertinent documentation—project management, design and development, recruitment—everything that in any way conveys or relays data and information that is project and operation related. He uses portable plug-in memory chips, similar to thumb drives of old, to store the artifacts.

He goes home every night and transfers the intelligence material on the chips to an e-dossier he maintains on his personal laptop. He backs it up to Cloud. Meanwhile, he continues work on a side project of his own. Intellectual input comes from his latest jottings, notes, and brainstorming ideas. It is his work ethic and instinct to be prepared for whatever comes next as well.

Kahtani calls an infamous Friday afternoon meeting. Friday afternoon and Monday morning meetings have been unwritten "don't-do's" for decades. They are shunned by all, and why

Kahtani does such a thing is disregarded before meeting start. It goes without saying. Mack is the only one who couldn't care less.

"Thank you all for breaking up your Friday plans to attend," Kahtani says to the seated team of managers. "Thank you."

Everyone silently forces a smile, more a grimace, back at him.

"The latest project plan terminates your contract and disallows further participation in the Advanced Energy project and current operation."

"What?" Hall asks, voice raising.

"Yah…" Cooper is visibly upset. "What the—"

"Must I repeat the news?"

"No," Mack replies. "I think they've got it."

"Your last day in residence here will be Friday, two weeks from today. You will be shuttled, compliments of the project upper management, back to your respective homes or any destination of your choice that Friday early evening."

"But why?" Charlie innocently asks.

"This is a next logical step in the sequence of events that bracket this effort.

This is not a reflection of your performance or behavior. Simply stated, your jobs here are done.

During the next two weeks, you will be working on a turnover to new oncoming junior operations managers.

King will remain with us a while longer, but the rest of you will be dismissed in fourteen days. All clear?"

17

Mofty turns over electronic metric, fundamental, comparison workbooks, a balance sheet, income statement, statements of changes in equity, statement of cash flows, and other financial tools and documents. Architectural specifications and a user guide are turned over with the software developed to generate all the pertinent metrics and audits. He also produces a set of specifications to hide, bury, and otherwise, keep Advanced Energy resources harvested under the radar: a deliverable that Kahtani, pleased, also has him deliver.

OPEC or the Organization of the Petroleum

Exporting Countries is an international organization headquartered in Vienna, Austria. It forms because the international oil market is largely dominated and mismanaged by a group of regulation-making multinational companies.

The formation of OPEC represents a collective act of sovereignty by most all major oil exporting nations and marks a turning point in state control over natural resources. OPEC ensures that oil companies cannot unilaterally cut or raise prices. Sometimes it works.

Its mandate is to coordinate and unify the petroleum policies of its members and to ensure the stabilization of oil markets in order to secure an efficient, economic, and regular supply of petroleum to consumers; a steady income to producers; and a fair return on capital for those investing in the petroleum industry. In that capacity, OPEC is largely successful.

OPEC crude oil production is an important factor affecting global oil prices. It sets production targets for its member nations, and generally, when OPEC production targets are reduced, oil prices increase. The oil-drilling boom in the United States increases oil production by over 70 percent and reduces the United States oil imports from OPEC by 50 percent. The introduction of the Advanced Energy effort, in full production to date and growing larger with time, reduces US oil imports to zero percent.

The United States absorbs the rapidly increasing domestic production of sweet, light, tight oil; and in one case, dramatically reduces like-for-like or similar grade imported crude oil from Nigerian and other African suppliers.

Crude oil prices occasionally and abruptly drop, most times by about a third as the

United States shale oil production increases and China's and Europe's demand for oil decreases. The United States confidently and rapidly backs out of the crude oil import market because of its own booming national production.

OPEC announces that America is the main non-OPEC oil supply contributor to an anticipated supply growth of 1.5 million barrels per day, to average 57.5 million barrels per day with advanced energy. The annual average price of oil was about US$140 per barrel. Since Advanced Energy, however, the price of oil slides to US$80. OPEC argues that this drop in the price of oil is not exclusively attributed to oil market fundamentals but has little more to offer on the phenomenon.

Along with the growth of advanced energy and global oversupply, appeals from the poorer OPEC member states that OPEC blocks stop and drop. More and more of OPEC member countries seek emergency OPEC meetings and joint coordination with the major players, such as Russia to stem a tumble in oil prices. Meetings come and go as oil prices continue to decline. Some call on OPEC to reduce oil output, suggesting cuts or a hold on production levels. OPEC policy to not cut production costs Saudi Arabia about $90 billion quarterly and nearly $700 billion a year for OPEC as a whole.

Leading oil financiers, let it be known that OPEC is effectively dissolved.

Like an exercise in connect the dots, each Advanced Energy site form an ever-developing and elongated fault line. Along and crossing the equator deep in the Atlantic, the man-made fault thread inadvertently links to a series of connected-to faults. These faults are so trivial that they go undetected.

Increases in seismic activity, ever so slight, appear on the scope. Mack sees also blips returned from the probes ahead that the same degree of significance resides along the chosen route. Since the activity preexists, there is no evidence of Advanced Energy being the cause.

Two-man submarines set off and motor down to the sites previously processed by Advanced Energy. They travel the line from the beginning and travel back toward the most recent site. All appears stable: there is no evidentiary indications on the ocean floor.

"Following detonation and what little hydraulic fracturing we do," Mack begins his oral status report, "seismic activity is almost certainly caused by the deep-injection disposal of hydraulic fracturing flowback. Flowback is a by-product of hydraulically fractured wells and produce formation brine, which is a by-product of both fractured and nonfractured oil and gas wells."

"Thank you, Mr. King." Kahtani's nerves are frayed. "Can you offer anything else on the subject before we move on?"

"Yes, all. It is for those reasons I mentioned that hydraulic fracturing is under international scrutiny, restricted in some countries, and banned altogether in others. Some countries have banned the practice or placed moratoria in place, while others have adopted an approach involving tight regulation. The European Union is drafting, as we speak, regulations that would permit only tightly controlled application of hydraulic fracturing.

That's all, sirs and madams."

$$\text{---}\!\!\ll\!\!\gg\ \textbf{18}\ \ll\!\!\gg\text{---}$$

Advanced Energy completes the project as planned and reverses course toward north-northeast. The lineup of new sites starts at the mid-North Atlantic Ocean, and forms a ζ line as it enters the northernmost South Atlantic Ocean. It travels farther south between the Americas and Africa. All entities of Advanced Energy are en route back to homeport, Norfolk, Virginia.

The submarines link to underwater tunnels that lead to an underground entryway into the Advanced Energy Norfolk Center. It is a combination of small-branch headquarters and a large operations technical hub. All project actors remain quartered there for three days and nights.

During their stay, they work with physical therapists and trainers to become grounded back on solid turf after such a long stretch of time underwater and cramped. They are reminded of the high and tight classification of the project they just completed. This is drilled into them categorically and pointedly, and explicitly as well, repeatedly.

During the exit interviews, the human resources manager provides them tickets to their respective homes or destinations. They are also rewarded with their pay. Curiously, payment comes in the way of a money order, along with $5,000 cash in a manila envelope.

Kahtani is here too. He handpicks a select few team members that meet his prerecorded criteria. He briefly describes the next project.

The option to participate and contribute is theirs. He tells those who choose to return to take eight weeks off and that they'll receive travel itineraries that will deliver them back to the hub. There is no further mention of project specificity. They will receive project-related introductory and educational essentials when they return.

The surprise at Rockall triggers exploration efforts of the Atlantic Ocean floor in and around the area. Researchers at the University of Lisbon create a new map of the seafloor, off the coast of Iberia—the region of Europe that includes Portugal and Spain—and the results show the beginnings of a new subduction zone. They continue outward to map the easternmost Atlantic and proceed toward the ocean's middle.

Mack keeps himself aware of the oceanic explorations by examining all reports produced as a result of the analysis of the ocean's floor. He shares nothing with Kahtani. His intuition has his belly aching, and his conscience renders anxiety—fear, uncertainty, and doubt. The FUD syndrome threatens to seep in.

The reports use the latest derived data extracted from the discoveries surrounding the subduction zones. They suggest what could happen when the tectonic plates—the large rock slabs that make up the earth's crust—crash into one another. The edge of the heavier plate slides or subducts below the lighter plate. It then melts back into the earth's mantle—the layer just below the crust.

A research vessel carries scientific oceanographers to a center point between Africa and South America. Research vessels are ships or large boats designed and equipped to carry out research at sea. The captain anchors just outside of the outer eastern edge of the Bermuda Triangle. Teleoperated robotics are employed by the researchers: they are the safest way to explore deepwaters. Remotely operated robotic vehicles, called ROVs, become the divers' and scientists' eyes and hands in deep-marine environments.

The ROV signals a fault present with slight seismic activity. Operators program a search-and-follow along the fault line. One ROV navigates north and one south. Both of them trace the fault line from both ends and plan to meet again at midpoint.

The ROVs signal movement detected. That is the last signal received from the two capsules. Operators above are baffled. Everyone is sick with worry: their first thought outlines the myths that spread about the queer disappearances within the Bermuda Triangle. Upper management on this scientific mission scoff and decide to act as smartly as possible. The exploratory leader orders electrode drop lines be used to note deepwater behavior below them.

The drop lines immediately return data showing water current. Analysts create readable informational reports from the raw data they continue to receive. The pull of the water is reminiscent of a whirlpool, but this is different from a single maelstrom. It is an elongated eddy that appears to be sucking hard from the fault line itself.

"Holy shit, look at this!" The senior scientist points at the latest report.

"My God, boss. What the heck?"

"Damn it," the top scientist yells. "Get me the most recent sys outs!" The system output constitutes the formatted reports he reads and uses.

"The line of vortex is actually rising," he dryly says.

"Sir," the second in command says, "we're picking up fault movement."

"What kind of movement?"

"It is in the midst of a widening from the midpoint out toward the sides and ends."

As the fault line widens, it causes an extraordinary pull from all sides into the crevice itself.

"Is this where the ROVs went?" the assistant asks.

"It's the best answer we've got at this time is that it does appear so… Shut up!"

The data abruptly stops coming up. This is an indication that the bulk of the movements that return data are either lower than the sensors or higher. The lead data entry professional hand delivers the latest notes to the scientists a floor up in the operations lab and office space.

"Wait," the top man says. "Do you feel that?"

"Yes, yes. What the is going on?"

"Stations, everyone! All hands on deck! All engines on! Full speed!

Captain! Take us due northeast!"

The large boat shakes in a fit of seizure at the stern as it begins to sink. The eddy current is stronger than the vessel engines. Those on deck see the most spectacular whirlpool motions they've ever imagined. The sea reflects the split happening way down: a black hole toward the floor.

Everyone on board is holding on tight as the bow rises slowly and the seawater rushes in and over everything and everyone from the stern forward. In one radical broad and sweeping motion, the boat disappears with a loud, vehement consumption intake sound—suction. Thirty minutes later, the fault along the Bermuda Triangle rests and settles where it's at, plates shifting with a cruiser boat wedged in between the side edges of plates.

Oceanic and coastal activities relate to the Advanced Energy-created faults, but Kahtani, eager to begin his self-defined phase two of the project, pays no attention and refuses to report the anomaly to his superiors. Without acknowledgement, they remain in the dark and, thus, uncaring as the team at sea executes their plan, and their efforts move forward. As far as the project sponsors are concerned, the effort is complete. They got what they paid for. Anything more that Kahtani can deliver is gravy.

As the Advanced Energy hardware team make the necessary augmentations according to the specifications delivered them, the South Atlantic fault elongates and encroaches northerly fifteen hundred miles in to the North Atlantic. The fault opens like a zipper. It travels up the line in a slow-moving wave. Just behind the crack-causing disturbance, another wave settles the large plates into newly disrupted positions, open fifty to one hundred yards wide.

The southeastern shores of Bermuda are lined with deadly undertow with extremely strong current pulling outward to the sea.

Shore erosion overnight destroys that side of the resort island. The beaches disappear, and the oceanside homes, hotels, museums, and churches crumble into the rushing sea. The material and human losses cannot yet be asserted. The entire island is vibrating. The terrified sixty-five thousand residents and the additional tourists are at a loss. Every survivor migrates to the northwestmost of Bermuda, which is already overcrowded with the fearful.

Volcanoes and earthquakes triggered throughout the Atlantic exacerbates the already dangerous circumstances around the world. Royal British Navy ships rove and weave through the mid-Atlantic searching for root cause. As the captain in one of them is signaled as they approach the fault line there, he stops the large vessel. He does not anchor yet but remains in place by utilizing the ship's jet systems.

Good old-fashioned sonar retrieves details about the fault line: its width, its depth, and an indicator of further length–in this case, either northerly or southerly. There is no further movement picked up, but clouded, murky sonograms indicate bizarre water movement of some kind. The captain and his technical team are able to agree on one thing about the movement: it is an extremely strong current drawing the sea into the opening.

Other recognizance ships located at the southernmost sign of the fault and at the northernmost sign of it, radio the awesome and awful *news* too. Albeit very slowly, the fault at both ends of the line continue to travel, breaking up plates and rearranging them some thirty-five yards apart, basically forecasting; thus, warning a runaway fault line as it develops. In no uncertain terms, the technical lead lays it out straight: basically, what is happening is the Atlantic

Ocean, the world, is splitting in two. They are witnessing a crack in the earth as it grows. We have a crack in the earth. It's cracking the nadir!

────── ✦ **19** ✦ ──────

Mack continues to read the reports. The discovery of the new subduction zone could eventually signal the start of an extended cycle that fuses continents together into a single landmass—or supercontinent—and closes the ocean. Upon further research, he learns that the breakup and reformation of supercontinents has happened at least three times during the earth's approximately three-billion-year history.

The scientists' discovery of the crack in the earth's crust decidedly conveys a threat to pull North America and Europe closer together. Depending on further conditions, such as additional widening of the fault line, this could indeed cause the Atlantic Ocean to vanish in no more than two million years, no less than two hundred years. Speaking confidentially with *National Geographic*, Mack documents that the earth's continents could "look very much like the Pangea" in the far future, referring to a supercontinent that existed about two hundred million years ago.

"Mr. King." Kahtani knocks on Mack's office door. "May I have a word?"

"Of course, Mr. Kahtani. Please sit down."

"Mr. King, you've performed admirably on the project. And that is an understatement."

"Well, thank you, Mr. Kahtani. And?"

"You are being dismissed from Advanced Energy. Your job, work here is done. Finished. And it has all been impeccable. The sponsors and I are exceedingly satisfied with all you contributed to the project."

"I see. And thank you. Thank you very much."

"Yes, and so I would like to set aside time to compare records on payments due to your consultancy and tie up any loose fray at either end."

"All right. Anytime is fine with me. I saw this coming weeks ago." Mack winks.

"There's no lead time necessary. We'll work with you, and you work with us. And as far as the project is concerned, you need not plan your departure around any given date."

"Okay."

"And we will honor and work around any leave date you have in mind. Fair enough?"

"Yes. That is fair. I am prepared to

leave as soon as you are ready to officially dismiss me."

"Well, Mr. King, I will set up an exit interview between HR and you and me as soon as I can."

"Excellent!"

"I'll be in touch soon."

"I'll be right here."

Mack sits at home at his desk making a chronological timeline report that captures every logically sequential event and decision within the Advanced Energy project. The paper, which serves as a cover page, is an overarching description of what the underlying report is about; it briefly introduces each and every topic expounded upon following.

The narrative is written in a hybrid

technical language style so as to reach every audience or readership member. He is masterful at writing perfectly clear technical elements commingled with business logic. It's a writing style that makes his report easily understood by all. He takes his time. There is no hurry or desperation. But he sets a loose due date for himself.

While contemplating the facts within the body of his report, Mack chooses a selective list of recipients. While the righteous and innocent professionals, politicians, and interested parties deserve and need to know the information he has to offer, he is careful not to include any sponsor, stakeholder, or other participant, colleague, player, or contributor on the now complete Advanced Energy project.

He sets forth no delivery date, although he is and will remain ready to share as soon as the time is right. The right time is constituted by the damage done that can be strictly tied to the project. He plans to caveat any other damage that in any way make the project suspect. He names the file "whistle."

Kahtani gets up from his desk and walks to his office door, locks it, and then goes over to his tan lateral steel cabinet. He unlocks and opens its bottom drawer, rifles through the hanging folder tabs, and lifts a manila envelope from the one labeled "Miscellaneous." A simple title on the front of the legal-sized envelope reads "Advanced Energy Exclusions."

He stares at the pouch, takes a deep breath, and then gingerly breaks the seal then bends the metal clamps outward. Kahtani reaches into the open slot and, without discern, pulls out the entire clipped packet of reports. He removes the large binder clip from the left-top corner and then fingers his way through the contents.

There are report titles across the top of each cover page. Kahtani rushes through his search and does not find what he is looking for. So he starts over, taking his time. Second to the last document packet, he notices it is not labeled. It is blank where there should be a title. He pulls it out and drops it on his desk. He looks at the last packet then clips them all together, returns them to the large envelope, reseals it, and locks it back into the lateral.

Kahtani feels the giddiness of a child on Christmas Eve as he lifts the packet from atop his desk. Although the cover page is not labeled with a title, he can tell what it is by skimming the contents therein. He begins to tremble, essential tremors of the guilty, confirming the subject from the short summary just read. It is analytic output that he maliciously and crookedly stole from Mackenzie King. It begins as such:

On Horizontal Drilling Beneath United States

Though perhaps not in the familiar liquid form—the ingredients are bound up in rock deep in the Earth's mantle. Discovery represents the planet's largest reservoir in existence. Researchers have found deep pockets of magma located beneath North America, namely the USA. The most excessive entry points specifically are along the mid-Atlantic seaboard. This is a likely signature of the presence of water at these depths as well. Simply stated, research shows that there sits a virtually limitless reservoir of magma below Northeast

America, perhaps between the lower mantle and the outer core.

Kahtani stops and reads the report's first page again. Then, breathing deeply, he finishes the brief yet concise document. He reads it a third time and resigns himself that it is all he needs to produce his own system analysis and thus introduce the project to the team he pulled together. The project, Advanced Energy: Phase Two, is unofficially launched as he finishes the first production document of many more to come.

20

Extensive development of volcanoes pop up around the Atlantic's triple junction of the Eurasian Plate, North American Plate, and the African Plate. The shallow earthquakes are associated with magmatic processes, yet the volcanoes are rare in many areas where there are earthquakes. The mid-Atlantic ridge, an extensive underground mountain range, has developed, and this is the site where the North American plate is moving and the Eurasian and African plates are moving . The result is a big scar down the center of the Atlantic Ocean where magma is rising up from the mantle to fill in the gap that is being created fighting the water to get down in it.

As the activity and movements continue, the fault line disastrously widened by Advanced Energy is active as well. The plates surrounding it shift and ease, falling into the line, causing deepwater swirls. Over three months, the movements cause the line to contract and abridge. Undertows and currents along the Atlantic shorelines slowly ease in concert with the compression of the man-originated fault line. Bermuda coast reconstruction begins.

Mack finishes reading the report and breathes a sigh of relief. The postevent investigations concentrate on the mid-Atlantic ocean floor: the small footprint of the Advanced Energy rigs to the south go unnoticed. The newly discovered fault line, just to the west, is recorded to be caused by the activity in the well-known triple junction. The new fault line zippers back together in much the same way that it unzipped but, this time, traveling north to south.

At the Norfolk branch labs, Kahtani busily crams the documentation together that describes and, in turn, initiates Advanced Energy: Phase 2. He gathers all the completed project's documentation to reuse as much as he can. There is a lot of doctoring to be done: he goes all the way back to the beginning, copying and editing, page by page, the entire project workbook.

Changing most is the analysis output, which will lean toward and revolve around horizontal drilling and encroachment and throughput. All the other phases are much or nearly all the same. The operator names must be changed throughout, along with the dialog supporting project summary, project scope, logical models, detailed analysis, and all the development documents. When that is complete, he summarizes, delineates, and describes operator responsibilities.

Nerves unraveled, Kahtani finds himself out of his element performing the research and analysis that identifies project production sites. Mack's high-level documentation, for instance, does not pinpoint the depth to which the penetration points shall reside. The continental shelf–Kahtani remembers the simple oceanographic fact–is the underwater landmass that extends from the coast in an area of relatively shallow water called the shelf sea. He takes to an encyclopedia for more.

The relatively accessible continental shelf is the best understood part of the ocean floor. Most commercial exploitation from the sea—such as metallic ore, nonmetallic ore, and hydrocarbon extraction—takes place on the continental shelf. Kahtani continues. The abyssal plain is the large area of extremely flat or gently sloping ocean floor just offshore from a continent at depths of thirteen thousand to twenty thousand feet. The abyssal plains begin where the continental margins end. Several species of worms, shrimp, brittle stars, sea cucumbers, and fish live in abyssal plains.

The continental margin, between the continental shelf and the abyssal plain, comprises a steep continental slope followed by the flatter continental rise. Sediment from the continent above cascades down the slope and accumulates as a pile of sediment at the base of the slope called the continental rise. Extending some 310 miles from the slope, it consists of thick sediments deposited by turbidity currents from the shelf and slope. The continental shelf and the slope make up the continental margin.

The shelf area is subdivided into the inner continental shelf, midcontinental shelf, and outer continental shelf, each with their specific geomorphology and marine biology. The character of the shelf changes dramatically at the shelf break, where the continental slope begins. The shelf break in its entirety is located at a remarkably uniform depth of roughly 460 feet.

The continental shelves are covered by terrigenous sediments, those derived from erosion of the continents. Sediments usually become increasingly fine with distance from the coast. Sand is limited to shallow wave-agitated waters while silt and clays are deposited in quieter deepwater far offshore.

Continental shelves teem with life because

of the sunlight available in their shallow waters in contrast to the biotic desert of the ocean's abyssal plain. Though the shelves are usually fertile, if anoxic conditions prevail during sedimentation, the deposits may, over geologic time, become sources for fossil fuels.

This is it!

This it!

This is what Kahtani is looking for. Now for the rights to that area awarded continents. Sovereign rights over their continental shelves extend to a distance where the depth of waters admitted of resource exploitation were claimed by the marine nations way back in the 1950s. But the 1982, United Nations Convention on the Law of the Sea created a two-hundred-nautical-mile-exclusive economic zone and extended continental shelf rights for states with physical continental shelves that extend beyond that distance.

Kahtani has his answer, but given project classification carried over from the original Advanced Energy project, he will go deeper with the probes and other apparatus. Horizontal drilling will be centered along coastal mid-Atlantic United States from New Jersey down through South Carolina. Kahtani disallows punctures in Florida and North Carolina, given the history of earlier attempts to produce oil and gas off both those states' coasts.

Moreover, he takes the mission two hundred miles farther out to sea, deeper under the selected continental margins' deepest point. Even though the drilling efforts completed decades ago identified best-case points of interest, Kahtani does not change his course of action and uses his documents that describe physical probing for reservoir indicators.

21

Mack's keen sense of intuition, less so than conscience, steers his evening's citing and detailing in totality the Advanced Energy project. He uses absolute copies of the project workbook as appendix source and addendum. He plans to put forth a powerful, pointed, alarming, horrifying, and shocking brief evidentiary record of testimony.

Where the Advanced Energy documentation began with and retained secrecy, Mack opens with and keeps at the forefront irrefutable and undeniable fact. He writes in the finest technical writing style but adds some anecdotal edge to reflect the arrogance under which all the actors so easily, without conscience, filled their roles.

He creates a one-page introduction, background, and summary that even in its consternation reads effortlessly and handily. Mack names the sponsor country's leaders and all the business-related project stakeholders below them. He maintains that Isaak Al Kahtani hatched the entire operation in plan but took a middle-management project role for the sake of reticence.

The brass reads like a who's who in the international oil industry and the United States government regulatory commissions. The system flow and accompanying narrative present simplicity so astonishing that the improbable looks like a comic book. Easily read, easily understood, and inconceivably horrid.

The preemptive body describes an operation that is too believable for it to cast doubt of any flavor. Who among that audience does not understand oil rigging—drilling for oil—fracking for shale and natural gas? But herein, who there has ever even dreamed of going to the deepest of all, hidden ocean floor, to excavate it?

So the introduction is intransigent; the operation is illustrated and recounted. So to finish the cover page, Mack publishes the throughput: the oil resources feed the West at a count of 32.5 million barrels a day. He explains the cracking in the nadir splitting the Atlantic in two, and finally, he announces Al Kahtani's presumably next steps. They must plan for proactive action, not reaction.

The inner galley of the report is an easy reading and illustrated walk-through of every site implementation, including the first failed live test at Rockall. It warns of underwater volcanoes, earthquakes, and rising tsunamis. Any one of these could conceivably impact many third world countries. Mack begins and ends his report, summarizing:

This document of truth shows the world that real scoundrel businessmen and world leaders know what they are doing–know where they are taking us and know what they are taking from us.The document goes on to express the concern over the great crack in the nadir. That discovery of the new subduction zone caused by the Advanced Energy project could eventually signal the start of an extended cycle that eventually but inevitably fuses continents together into a single landmass– or supercontinent–and closes the ocean. He cites scientific evidence that the breakup and reformation of supercontinents has happened at least three times during earth's approximately three-billion-year history.

The crack in the earth's crust decidedly conveys the threat to pull North America and Europe closer together. This is not theory; it is fact. Additional widening of the fault line could indeed cause the Atlantic Ocean to vanish in no more than two million years, no less than two hundred years. Finally, Mack documents that earth's continents could "look very much like the Pangea," in the future, referring to a supercontinent that existed about two hunded million years ago.

Mack spends days pouring over his report, proofing, editing, and formatting. He is undecided about timing; but now that it is an expert-level affidavit, all that's left are the mailing labels. He's going straight back to his old pal at the Pentagon, a few high-ranking committee members in the House and Senate, and in almost an award, a trusted friend in the media who is the earth and science editor at *National Geographic*.

Kahtani's dismissal of King marks a finish line for him, but certainly not for Mack. Cracking the nadir is now well-cited in detail: it can ship anytime, but there is something else burning inside. Mack has not forgotten the hushed conversation when he, in admittedly bad form, discloses the reservoirs that lie under the eastern North American territories. He looks down at his two hands and counts the age spots that have slowly appeared over the past few years.

This effort is much more difficult to detail, not so much in that the reservoirs do exist but when and where Al Kahtani will strike the coastline. There is no doubt in Mack's mind that he will, and Mack wants Al Kahtani caught in action, but before the most severe danger threatens to occur. Mack requests a meeting with the CIA.

Al Kahtani's second phase components of Advanced Energy are all in place. This time, he works on each site concurrently instead of serially. The blasting and probing trigger the reopening of the fault line: the crack in the nadir widens again. The process is slow but eventual and imminent. The strong undertows can be felt along the entirety of the North American east coast and the coasts of Great Britain, Ireland, Spain, Portugal and all but destroy the islands that dot the northernmost European Atlantic Ocean coast all the way to Northwest Africa.

The horizontal drilling under the States decimate the shelf: it is destructed and crushed. The pull continues to draw the crumbled seascape down and out to the crack in the nadir. Even the tide seems to be rolling out instead of into the beach from the Jersey Shore down to South Carolina.

The farther out the eradication travels with the underwater rush, a truculent, warlike progression forms and grows as a combative line reaching colossal annihilation. The United States' east coast falls into and out with the seas. The fault created by Advanced Energy widens as more and more pressure shoves the plates apart.

The undercurrent and whirlpools trigger havoc in the Atlantic, including hundreds of miles of littoral landmasses. Islands in Mid-Atlantic from the outside in literally dissolve. Material items are moderately sucked outward, toward the center ocean.

The strength grows by the week, and by the end of the month, Mack's professional partners begin to call. Political and powerful influences demand explanation of circumstances around the world. He responds with two statements. The project scoundrels are now falling victim to their own creation through their own greed.

"Basically, what is happening is the world is splitting in two by the mammoth and tremendous crack in the nadir caused by Advanced Energy. I urge you to study the first whistle-blower report I released. But I sent a second insider's report to you all in overnight mail. It explains what and why the US Atlantic coastline is disappearing faster than anywhere else on either side of the Atlantic coast.

"I am prepared to turn state's and federal evidence of the Advanced Energy project crimes *and* tie it to the global catastrophes by virtue of the two reports, additional project documentation, and eyewitness accounts. I am certain some or all of my project teammates will step forward with me. But we must get to them before Al Kahtani does. I am certain he will kill them…and me.

"All the evidence logically and precisely explains the entire root cause and expected result of the projects, besides the obvious and much sought-after crude, gas, shale, and coal."

Mack is exhausted and decides to order Chinese delivery. It takes longer than usual but arrives in about ninety minutes. He is hungry and wolfs it down fast. It is good but tastes like they put an extra tablespoon of MSG in it or something! A nutty taste. He laughs inside at himself and finishes. He lies down on the couch.

— ❧ 22 ❧ —

The note opened in TextPad on Mack's laptop reads, I am so, so sorry, and I beg God's forgiveness.

I am so exhausted.

I can no longer stand the

pain

sadness

loneliness

crying

mania

depression

rejection

I tried so hard with doctors, medication, and people. Nothing has worked. I have not felt peace or joy since my divorce.

Doctors—I intentionally overdosed on alcohol, sleeping pills, sedatives, and antidepressants.

I am going to lie on the couch to die.Soon Mack finds himself sinking into a deep sleep on the couch, or bed.

Where am I?

He floats fourteen inches off the couch.

Not going toward the light; the light is approaching him.

He sees flashes of familiar images of Christ and his own parents and ancestral family within a lightly colored and filtered vista.

The language he hears is one not immediately

understood—is it in tongues? Wait. It sounds kind of like Latin.

Magically, his mindfulness can interpret the message—the words—spoken in perfect English, more his native language.

*Mackenzie, we have been close for a long, long time. I am here to intervene and assure you your sins are forgiven.*He takes Mack's right hand and holds it.

An appendage comes forth from the light and makes circular motions above Mack's diaphragm. He sees a circle of white with black specks over his abdomen.

The Spirit is cleansing your soul with God's pure white grace from heaven. See how white your soul is, Mackenzie. The blackness is gone.

Your search for the love of your life shall cease; it one day shall come. Please know that one day, a good, decent Christian woman will recognize you and realize your gifts—she joins you. We shall not, at this point, assess your other concerns for which you pray. Leave them be, Mackenzie. Leave them be.

We know you were born with many purposes in life. Your achievements and accomplishments are obvious. Your guilt lies within a love so deep it has become the one purpose you look beyond.

I know that you know, through life reflection and soul-searching, have encountered those purposes of life. Yet the one that escapes you is the one closest to you: the earth, all things, and all beings—yes, but first and foremost, your children. You are full of love, Mackenzie. Share it.

Follow me as God asked of man to follow

him. You may follow in your path that I have provided you.

Just remember your blood code—B Positive.

Use any tool you need to worship, in group or not, but know the answer always lies somewhere in the church of the soul, temple of the spirit, and the love in your heart. Teach your children this: to follow my path. The simple path of love. It is that simple. That is your purpose.

*I will tell you when it is time to die!*A soft and soothing woman's voice instructs him.

*Listen for the angels singing.*At that precise point, the phone rings, and Mack snaps back on the couch.

The woman introduces herself then asks out of the blue, "Are you depressed?"

"Yes."

"Do you feel you could hurt yourself?"

"I already did."

Mack wakes in the hospital. He hears the doctor say he does not understand how the patient lived. He should be dead. He *was* dead for some moments.

"I can hear you, you know."

"Nurse! Gather the team! Can you hear me, Mr. King?"

"Yes. I think so."

"Your attempted suicide failed, sir. But we are all here to help you."

"Suicide? Suicide?"

"Yes, Mr. King," an officer of the law says.

"We read your note. We found the empty alcohol and pill vials."

"I didn't attempt suicide!"

"Denial is typical, Mr. King. It's okay. It's all right." The nurses voice is so sweetly soothing.

"No, Doctor, you don't understand. I did *not* attempt suicide! I ate some bad-tasting Chinese food and began to feel woozy. I lay on the couch and experienced a very clear and vivid dream. *I swear on my father's grave*, I did *not* attempt suicide. I implore you to investigate this further." Mack falls back asleep.

The doctors take a blood screening, and Mack wakes and yells when a male nurse runs a catheter up through his urethra. Mack feels as ill as he ever has. His entire body hurts: every bone feels like it is shattered, and every muscle feels pulled.

He feels more awake with every moment. The nurses remain in the room with him, and Mack starts a conversation with one of them.

"Can you tell me what exactly is going on here?"

"I'm sorry, Mr. King, but no. We can't."

"Why do they think I attempted suicide?"

"I can repeat what you've already heard," the male nurse begins. "An anonymous caller to 911 reported you needed help. The attending medics found you barely conscious, and at one point in the ambulance, you expired. The police officers that answered the call with the medics brought in the empty bottles and pill vials, and they have your laptop computer with a suicide note opened on the desktop."

"To be clear," Mack says, "I was brought in pronounced dead but was resuscitated somehow, and because of the note and the empty vials, it is assumed that I attempted to kill myself. Right?"

"That is correct, Mr. King."

"And now they are running my blood and my urine to confirm that I actually did ingest what was in the vials…"

"Yes, sir."

"Okay. Thank you." Mack falls asleep again.

When he awakes, he asks to speak to the police. The memories of details during the timeline until his collapse are coming back.

"May I please speak to the police?" Mack asks the nurse.

"Sir, everything and everyone is on hold until we receive the test results."

"I tell you, man—this is of the utmost importance."

"The best I can do is relay your request to him. I'm sure he'll want to talk to you anyway, but I'll tell him."

"Thank you."

"Officer," the doctor calls.

"Yes. What have you got?"

"There aren't any traces of the medications that are labeled on those vials. But something else came up in the all-encompassing poisonous blood work we typically do, especially when the patient is adamant in his word or display obvious symptoms.

"Listen, Officer…we found a lethal dose of potassium cyanide poison."

"Holy shit! This guy *is* shootin' us straight!"

"Yes, well, we'll be keeping him here for

at least seven to ten days to administer the antidotal treatments and for observation. I am compelled to remind you that, although I realize an investigation is in order, please respect the man and give him plenty of resting time…please."

"Of course, Doctor," the officer replies. "I'm going to have to call in our forensics unit."

The medical team and law officers spend the afternoon in a meeting. Everyone must be and stay on the same page, the correct page. From the medical side, the most importance is placed upon the healing process. From the lawful point of view, intoxication is at the top of the list.

"What are the effects of potassium cyanide poison on a human?" the law starts things off.

"Some of the symptoms that occur when

that happens and all sorts of different things can or will happen…

"Patients will, first of all, notice there'll be this faint almond smell, and that's sort of important because that's probably the only sort of distinguishing characteristic of cyanide. It's hard to taste otherwise. It's hard to smell otherwise besides the faint almond. People feel dizzy, perhaps initially experience convulsions, or perhaps seizures, and some foaming at the mouth. That foaming at the mouth is sort of what people typically think of when they think of a cyanide poisoning. Movies…

"And finally, complete organ shutdown occurs, and then death. People, we caught this man right on that cusp!" the doctor exclaims.

"And how accessible is it to the public?" the lead doctor wants to know.

"You know," the forensic scientist says, "it's remarkably easy to purchase cyanide online as well as obtain several other highly toxic substances. These are substances you can easily buy on chemical websites, other websites—Jesus, all sorts of things.

"In fact, we had some undercover agents right here in town—just for our own little internal test—to try and do it themselves. They actually clicked on potassium cyanide. It tells you it's toxic. It shows a skull and crossbones icon next to the product image. And then it gives you a price. I think this one was about $110. And you can quite easily click it, purchase it, and have it sent right to your home." The forensics man sighs.

"Potassium cyanide," the commanding officer continues, "it is a substance that people have known about for a long time to be very toxic. So you can just see, we did it ourselves. You can see how easy it is to buy cyanide, along with several other toxic substances."

"Yes," the doctor continues. "And cyanide is actually found in a lot of products that most people probably don't even consider."

"Yes," the officer says. "We looked to see where else you could find cyanide, other places you might find it. We compiled a list, I believe, of some various places where cyanide is indeed found and used. Common places, like pesticides, metal strippers, metal-plating solutions.

"And bear in mind that you can buy that sort of stuff at, you know, hardware stores, hobby shops, electronics stores, places like that. The most remarkable thing, Doc, as you may not know, is you don't need an ID to buy any of that. A teenager, certainly a kid, could go in there and buy any of that stuff and take it home. And there you could have quite a bit of cyanide on hand."

"I want to explain to you why it took five days in that case three years ago for the person essentially to die."

"Cyanide is something that people have studied for a long time. Everyone heard about it with the Tylenol poisonings about 1978 and the Jim Jones poisonings, also back in 1978. What happens when someone contracts a cyanide poisoning is that it absolutely interferes with *all* of the body's ability to intake oxygen. So none of the cells in the body are getting *any* oxygen.

"As far as that particular case—five days— that is probably a bit unusual. Usually cyanide will veritably kill much more quickly than that. We're talking about hours here.

"Here's what happens when someone goes to

the hospital: The staff is going in reality to try and support that person by putting them on a ventilator to try to give them oxygen back. They're probably going to try a medication to get the body to rid itself of the cyanide. Sometimes that works well, sometimes not as well, sometimes not at all. We pump the stomach for all the obvious reasons. If there's cyanide in the stomach, we've got to pump it.

"But when a person comes into the hospital with cyanide poisoning, it's pretty unusual. First, we've got to figure out that's what it is and then do those things just stated. No matter what this guy had, we knew we had to pump first. That helped him get to this point."

"Five days is a little bit of a long time," the scientist mentions, referring to an old cyanide poisoning case.

"Probably what happened in that boy's case is that his organs just gradually shut down, yet ultimately, extraordinarily quickly, and he subsequently died with really no recourse for our doctors or the hospital.

"I have a detailed handout for your reading interest. There's no need to talk through it all when you can walk through it yourself—with this," the lead doctor concludes and hands out the packet.

"Happy reading, Officers!"

Potassium Cyanide Poisoning

Administer a cyanide antidote if the diagnosis of cyanide toxicity is strongly suspected without waiting for laboratory confirmation. Available antidotes are hydroxocobalamin, also known as Cyanokit, and sodium thiosulfate and sodium nitrite, also known as Nithiodote. Both are given intravenously.

Patients who present with more than minimal symptoms that resolve without treatment should be admitted for observation and supportive care. In patients with acute poisoning from hydrogen cyanide (HCN) gas or soluble salts, the principal acute care concerns are hemodynamic instability and cerebral edema. The continuous cardiac monitoring, respiratory and cardiovascular support, and frequent neurologic evaluation these patients require is generally best provided in an intensive care unit.

Conversely, acute poisoning from cyanogens, also known as nitriles or poorly soluble salts, may not manifest or become life-threatening for several hours after exposure. These patients require a 48-hour observation period.

Oxygenation should be optimized and continuous cardiac monitoring provided. Depending on the severity of symptoms, endotracheal intubation may be necessary to optimize oxygen delivery and protect the airway. Serum lactate concentrations, chemistries, and arterial or venous blood gases should be monitored.

Patients should be reevaluated 7–10 days after discharge from the hospital. Delayed onset of Parkinson-like syndrome or neuropsychiatric sequelae may be noted on follow-up.

The doctor and officers enter Mack's room. The doctor speaks first.

"Mr. King, we found a lethal dose of potassium cyanide in your system. We're going to take the proper actions as soon as the officers here are finished for the day. They will not be long.

"Will you, officers…"

"No. Mr. King, please tell us first, are you aware of anyone who may want to kill you, want you dead?"

"Officers, please listen to me. This is much, much bigger than you and me. And your answer is *yes*."

"Mr. King, please..."

"No! You listen to me. There are other people in danger as well. And for many classified—soon to be unclassified—reasons, I must get through to the Pentagon. This is a *must*. It is *paramount*. I must quickly confide with a representative high governmental official who represents me. It *is* that important. Please get me a phone. Please! Then I promise to answer all your questions and tell you anything you want to know. But this person in DC must know first. He must be told NOW. This a global issue!"

The cops aren't quite sure what to do. This man is commanding and, for a guy stricken with cyanide poisoning, very clear, concise, and knowing. One of them leaves to get a phone.

"Chuck! Chuck! It's Mack. Listen. I'm in the hospital. I've been poisoned—it was an attempted murder. Yes, I'm all right now. I have to make this quick. I've got cops in here I have to debrief, but you have to know first. Please open both packages I sent you ASAP. Plan for action. You'll know what to do. Meanwhile, I'll need to remain here a few more days. There is an addendum following the second packet. I am receiving anonymous death threats. The described project's security team vows to kill me if I blow the whistle or testify. They demand I recant all specificity from my reports—sent to you and a few others—and testimony. Please dig deep and hard into the two reports I just sent to you. I'll be in touch. Please take Joan Dempsey and Omar El Mofty in and under guard. If the others, Hall, and Cooper are alive, take them in too! Bye for now. I'll be in touch!"

III
SOLITARY REFINEMENT

Chuck sends a small squad of Secret Service agents to Mack's New Jersey home with instructions on what to retrieve and deliver. They bring his attaché hidden under some bedroom floorboards, a duffle bag with a change of clothes, a small suitcase full of cash, his phone, watch, and weapons. He is holed up in a location in Mahwah Township, usually reserved for high-level political figures. It is quiet. It is safe. It is hidden.

He intends to right the wrongs he took part in and then take it further. Mack reviews the Biomass Report that he started months ago. He performs additional analysis over different alternate sources of energy. It has to be renewable, nonpollutant, inexpensive from the bottom-up and easily harvested. He believes the answer lies in some form of biofuel or biomass energy. He also includes theories involving geothermal and hydro sources.

He begins his thesis: "Biomass is biological material derived from living or recently living organisms. It most often refers to plants or plant-derived materials that are specifically called lignocellulosic biomass. As an energy source, biomass can either be used directly via combustion to produce heat, or indirectly after converting it to various forms of biofuel.

"Conversion of biomass to biofuel can be achieved by different methods that are broadly classified into thermal, chemical, and biochemical methods. Wood remains the largest biomass energy source; examples include forest residues–such as dead trees, branches and tree stumps, yard clippings, wood chips, and even municipal solid waste. He states the intent to keep clear from live forests.

"In the second sense, biomass includes plant or animal matter that can be converted into fibers or other industrial chemicals, including biofuels. Industrial biomass can be grown from numerous types of plants, including miscanthus–any tall perennial bamboo-like grass of the genus *Miscanthus*, native from Southern Africa to SE Asia–switchgrass, hemp, corn, poplar, willow, sorghum, sugarcane, bamboo, and a variety of tree species, ranging from eucalyptus to oil palm.

"Bottom line: plant energy is produced by crops specifically grown for use as fuel that offer high biomass output per hectare with low-input energy. Some examples of these plants are wheat, which typically yield 7.5–8 tons of grain per hectare, and straw, which typically yield 3.5–5 tons per hectare in the UK. The grain can be used for liquid transportation fuels while the straw can be burned to produce heat or electricity. Plant biomass can also be degraded from cellulose to glucose through a series of chemical treatments, and the resulting sugar can then be used as a first-generation biofuel.

"Biomass can be converted to other usable forms of energy like methane gas or transportation fuels like ethanol and biodiesel. Rotting garbage and agricultural and human waste all release methane gas–also called landfill gas or biogas. Crops, such as corn and sugarcane, can be fermented to produce the transportation fuel, ethanol.

"Biodiesel, another transportation fuel, can be produced from left-over food products like vegetable oils and animal fats. Also, biomass to liquids and cellulosic ethanol are still under research.

"Bottom line: there is a great deal of research involving algal fuel or algae-derived biomass due to the fact that it's a nonfood resource and can be produced at rates 7 to 10 times those of other types of land-based agriculture, such as corn and soy. Once harvested, it can be fermented to produce biofuels such as ethanol, butanol, and methane, as well as biodiesel and hydrogen.

"The biomass used for electricity generation varies by region. Forest by-products, such as wood residues, are common in the United States. Agricultural waste is common in Mauritius in sugarcane residue and Southeast Asia: rice husks. Animal husbandry residues, such as poultry litter, are common in the United Kingdom.

"Biofuels include a wide range of fuels that are derived from biomass. The term covers solid, liquid, and gaseous fuels. Liquid biofuels include bioalcohols, such as bioethanol and oils, such as biodiesel. Gaseous biofuels include biogas, landfill gas, and synthetic gas. Bioethanol is an alcohol made by fermenting the sugar components of plant materials, and it is made mostly from sugar and starch crops. These include maize, sugarcane, and more recently, sweet sorghum.

"Bottom line: the latter crop is particularly suitable for growing in dryland conditions and is being investigated by International Crops Research Institute for the Semi-Arid Tropics for its potential to provide fuel, along with food and animal feed, in arid parts of Asia and Africa.

"With developing advanced technology, cellulosic biomass, such as trees and grasses, are also used as feedstocks for ethanol production. Ethanol can be used as a fuel for vehicles in its pure form, but it is usually used as a gasoline additive to increase octane and improve vehicle emissions. Bioethanol is widely used in the United States and in Brazil. The energy costs for producing bioethanol are almost equal to the energy yields from bioethanol.

"Bottom line: biofuels do not address global warming concerns.

Biodiesel is made from vegetable oils, animal fats, or recycled greases. It can be used as a fuel for vehicles in its pure form or, more commonly, as a diesel additive to reduce levels of particulates, carbon monoxide, and hydrocarbons from diesel-powered vehicles. Biodiesel is produced from oils or fats using transesterification and is the most common biofuel in Europe. Biofuels provided 2.7% of the world's transport fuel in 2020.

"Biomass, biogas, and biofuels are burned to produce heat and power and, in doing so, consequently, harm the environment. Pollutants such as sulphurous oxides, nitrous oxides, and particulate matter are produced from the combustion of biomass. The World Health Organization estimates that seven million premature deaths are caused each year by air pollution. Biomass combustion is a major contributor.

"Bottom line: the life cycle of the plants is sustainable, the lives of people less so."

Mack is satisfied with the fact address and saves it as the lead-in summary and background on the subject. He has an acceptable introduction to his Biomass Report. Due to the soil qualities, available land expanse, the ease, climate, the inexpensive and available accessibility, he begins the base of his revelation in the publication.

He paraphrases the detailed description of existing widespread and expanding solutions, such as wind, hydro, solar, and geothermal energies. These remain and flourish regardless of the biomass elucidation that follows.

Introducing hempseed and oil, Mack forms the affinity to China, the world's first papermaker. They used hemp to make paper 1,900 years ago. Both the Gutenberg Bible and the King James Bible were printed on hemp-based papers. In addition to paper, hemp can be used for edible oil, automotive oil, cooking and heating fuel, fabric, medicine, and construction beams.

Hemp's fiber length and strength make it optimal for replacing old-growth forest fibers in high-quality papers. Hemp hurds produce four times the paper per acre as wood. Hemp paper is a renewable industrial raw material and is environmentally friendly. Wood pulp is processed with hydrogen peroxide where wood-based paper is processed with sulfuric acid. The wood-pulp process is a major industrial pollutant while hemp pulp is almost pollution-free.

Hemp paper is stronger, acid-free, has a longer shelf life, and costs less than half as much to process as wood-based paper. Hemp paper can be recycled ten times where wood-based paper can only be recycled twice without losing integrity and requiring additional virgin fiber content.

In closing, Mack writes, hemp primary fiber is an excellent raw material for a range of products including recycled-paper strengthening, filter paper, currency and bond paper, high-quality document paper, handmade paper, clothing, lightweight concrete, pressboard, PVC, and wood-flour products.

He injects a few facts about a long-standing American resource: cotton. Philadelphia's "Rittenhouse" Paper Mill, the first paper-manufacturing facility in the United States, made recycled paper from cotton rags. Peddlers traveled the New England states regularly, buying old cotton rags from people's homes to make into paper. Cotton paper mills still flourish in the United States today, making high-end fine papers. In fact, US currency is made from cotton and flax.

Most cotton pulp comes from cotton linters, short clippings that are a residue left from secondary ginning by seed-oil companies after the longer fibers are removed from cotton bolls for fabric. Some cotton-paper manufacturers are using clippings from organic cotton-clothing mills to avoid pesticides. Cotton can also be mixed with other recycled-paper fiber for a high-quality paper type. Uses include paper, clothing, and potentially clean oil fuel.

Mack expounds upon an obscure but existing crop called kenaf. Beginning in the 1950s, the US Department of Agriculture evaluated hundreds of fiber crops and determined that kenaf was the best option for tree-free papermaking in the United States. The fact that kenaf fibers have many similarities to wood fibers increased its potential adaptability to the current mill system. At present, kenaf is an expensive option, but only due to its lack of economy of scale.

This could quickly change with increased demand.

Related to hibiscus, kenaf is a fast-growing plant that can be harvested annually over several months then compressed and stored for up to four years. It grows in the southern United States and yields far more fiber per acre than a comparable-size tree plantation. Pulping kenaf requires less energy than pulping wood, and it is more easily bleached with totally chlorine-free processes. Kenaf has great possibility as an environmentally sustainable crop that can bring new life to rural economies. Uses include paper and potentially renewable fuel.

Flax is one star of the show. It is characterized by very long high-quality fibers that are ideal for papermaking due to their strength and bonding properties. Flax oil or linseed oil is utilized in a number of alternative flooring materials. With additional milling, the oil may be used as renewable energy fuel. Flax produces fibers of varying length and, as a consequence, is suitable for many end products. Flax can be cultivated in the north in course soil, such as Maine and other New England states and west from there. An example Mack cites is Ireland, where the earth is very similar to that of Maine, USA: Flax flourishes. Uses beyond biofuel currently include clothing and draperies, furniture, canvas, geotextiles, paper, sacking, and flooring.

The last but most potential biofuels are algal fuel or algae-derived fuel due to the fact that it's a nonfood resource and can be produced at rates five to ten times those of other types of land-based agriculture. Once harvested, it can be fermented to produce biofuels such as ethanol, butanol, and methane, as well as biodiesel and hydrogen.

Bioethanol is an alcohol made by fermenting the sugar components of plant materials, and it is made mostly from sugar and starch crops. These include maize, sugarcane, and more recently, sweet sorghum. These crops are particularly suitable for growing in dryland conditions. They hold hidden, however likely capability–promise–for fuel production.

Mack closes with a topline list each devoted to the resolutions explained. He proofs the article three times, sleeps the night, then calls Chuck first thing in morning and instructs the delivery process for the all-important report.

──────── ❧❦ **24** ❦❧ ────────

In the pouring rain, a long black rain topcoat
and hat hide him well as he is escorted into
the cabin of the train. He sits with eyes
closed but wakes within a couple hours.
Mack thinks as the Amtrak streaks through
Baltimore that the house is empty and on
the market. He has a black Jag and a black
Yukon: he has his son sell the two vehicles
and keep the money, or keep the vehicles if
he wishes. The young man shortly has a large
roll of cash in his right pocket and his new
car keys in his left. Mack knows that there
are corrupt authorities looking for him, and
thinking of an old episode of *The Fugitive*

reminds Mack that to groom a little cosmetic change was inevitable and would be told so by the attorneys and detectives regardless.

Mack stares into the petite scratched mirror, the steady ride of the train desensitizing the rider from the vibrations and bumps that otherwise remain built-in. It's hinged and toggled to the stainless steel medicine cabinet bolted to the half-bath wall. It shakes along with the ride, yet against the view of the user.

Mack decides to go for the hair first because he thinks it might be easier than the beard. He's not sure why he thinks that since he hasn't cut his hair in over ten years. Beard trimming is a multistep, multitool, and major production; he does know based on more recent experience. He does all he can to put off or avoid putting the scissors near his face.

Pulling the long ponytail out from under his collar, the locks naturally twist around his arm. He remembers the morning two years before when he decided to tuck it into his shirt for the big-job appearances—interviews. Whenever someone around him asks the familiar "Just how long is your hair anyway?" question, the stock answer is always, "My hair is so long I've got to part it to sit."

Those days are gone. Reaching up to the nape of the neck with his left hand, the hair encircled within grip, it swirls and twists around his arm as he pulls downward and across to the right side. Standing in the moment, there before the mirror, left arm forming a hair-enrobed shield across his chest, he feels the snip should come easy. But it doesn't. Mack's right hand cramps and thumb knuckle throbs with sharp pain as his scissors jaggedly tear and break the hair away with every mouth, gnawing up and down.

when finally, the tail breaks free, Mack trims straight and then shakes loose the hair that remains on his head. He lowers the thumb from his mouth, having sucked the pain out that was killing him moments before. He considers the look before him again, and it strikes him. He likes what he sees. It's cool looking. It's tightly undone. He doesn't change a thing. He's acutely aware that any rendering used by the police or others would include varying hairstyles and lengths as he applies the gel and slicks it back. It looks like Vincent's from *Pulp Fiction*. It looks darker, almost black, like his mom's used to be when she was a young woman.

The bearded variations of face Mack entertained off and on throughout his ten years in the tank of science revolve around an ever-present goatee. However, the beard is full and big after his two years in submergence for Advanced Energy. After getting as close as he is able to with the shears, Mack engages the razor. Eight failing cartridges later, face burning red, Mack is rid of it all, including the goatee. If not for the Garcia T-shirt, and without the blue veiny nose, he'd look like an alcoholic Wall Street suit.

Once again taken by the image in the mirror, Mack is stuck in an unrecognizing stare. It's not him. He knows it's not any flavor of Mack seen since childhood, no matter who's doing the looking. Lo and behold, hark and be hush—he had forgotten about this—there is a huge cleft in the center of his chin. Running all the way from the top of the chin, just below the bottom-lip undercrease, to the bottom of it, its depth increased toward the middle and tapered toward the poles.

Chin hair covered the vertically elongated dimple ever since adolescence, so it would be well forgotten by now. The gape wasn't prominent back then, Mack remembers, but was visible.

My, it's grown!

This could represent an asset or a liability. His mind's wheels turn faster, seemingly than do those under the train, and he absently rinses his face with hot water. He repeats using the cold. Red spots of blood sprout. Reaching for the towel to hold against it, he is suddenly jarred into the wall. The towel hook bruises his right shoulder, and in an awakening, arrival comes already in Greenville.

From the Amtrak station, Mack is delivered to Donaldson Air Force Base, which is a former facility of the United States Air Force located south of Greenville, South Carolina. It was founded in 1942 as Greenville Army Air Base; it was deactivated in 1963 and converted into a civilian airport. From here, Mack switches vehicles inside a closed hangar and is then motored back north, only to land at a cheap motel all the way into the busy center of Atlantic Beach.

"Mack…" It's Mack's attorney, John Gianfacaro.

"John." Mack is surprised. "It's good to see you…here." They do a man hug.

"Well, I've got to make certain this package is tied up all nice and pretty, you know."

Mack chuckles. "Thanks for that, John."

"Mack, this is Jake McGhee, personnel, Pentagon. Your buddy Chuck sent him down special to get this thing done. He's the best, Mack."

"And what exactly is this thing?"

"Mack, Jake will be assigning you your

new identity and all that comes along with that. You're going into WitPro...the Witness Protection Program. Just relax for a while. That was a long trip by rail. Jake will start processing and bring you into the conversation when the time is right."

"Okay, guys," Mack says. "I could use a little rest."

Mack wakes late the following morning. There is coffee and doughnuts waiting there in the kitchenette for him. John gives Mack a few minutes to turn out for the day.

"Good Morning, Mack."

"Morning...what time is it? Heck. What day is it?" Mack chuckles along with John. They hear Jake softly laugh from the small round table, where he is nose-down busy working on something. He looks to be slowly and deliberately laying out an assortment of paperwork and documents. It looks like a cosmic game of solitaire.

"My new credentials?" Mack whispers to John.

"Why don't you shower up, get dressed, and then we'll get down to the business at hand," John suggests.

"Sounds good. Exactly what I need."

Jake looks up, rubbing the back of his neck. He's been hunched over the tabletop for nearly ninety minutes. "Ah, finally."

"Everything in order?" John asks Jake.

"I believe so. I've gone over it all twice since laying it all out."

"Excellent. Thank you, Jake."

"John, please. This is what I do." Jake grins.

"Right." John smiles.

Mack gets dressed, gently massages soothing balm into his raw face, and combs his hair back. "Where are my bags?" he asks John.

"Well, Mack…everything begins anew today. Everything, even your bags. Your outfit for the day is in the duffle. I hope you're satisfied with it."

"I'm sure it'll be fine. I'm catching on here."

"Okay, Mack, sit down here next to me," Jake calls.

"Sure. What do we have here?" Mack sarcastically asks.

"Mackenzie King, you are now and hereby one *Richard C. Baldwin*."

"What's the C—"

"Charles," Jake answers before Mack can get the question out.

Jake hands Mack a steno pad and pencil. He suggests Mack jot questions, comments, and concerns as the walk-through occurs. They'll address them all at once when Jake completes the initial readout.

"Okay," Jake says. "Are we ready?"

"Let's go," Mack says.

Jake begins and moves along slowly, making eye contact with Mack as he works through everything. He pushes the different documents to Mack as he announces what they reference or represent.

"Introducing the new you:

"Richard Charles Baldwin, here's your driver's license, social security card, birth certificate, and passport—everyday personal credentials.

"Birthplace: Limerick, Maine."Saint Joseph's College of Maine: Standish, Maine."PhD in English Literature."Author and freelance writer."Home address: 88 Ridley Lane, Litchfield, Maine."Your total net worth is twenty-three million dollars and growing."Funds representing your disposable income lie in a money market checking account at Sabattus Regional Credit Union."Revolving monthly balance at SRCU will be held at one hundred thousand dollars."Source transferred quarterly from Fidelity to SRCU."Retirement, investments, and dividends held at Fidelity, Portland, Maine—growing incrementally fast."If you play 'em right, Baldwin, your grandkids' grandkids won't have to work."Parents Ralph and Mary deceased in an automobile accident shortly after Richard's birth—that's you."Only-child Richard was raised in a foster home in Brunswick, Maine."New Social Security card with a new number, perpetual passport with visa; State of Maine–issued driver's license, motorcycle included–I gave to you."Now, use this bank card from SRCU exclusively. Do not introduce any other creditors."Private health, dental and vision insurance policy under Careington insurance."Jake pushes the short stack of documents over to Mack.

"Brand-new home is an oversized ranch-style, thirty-five thousand feet, 77' × 42'."It is a log home with flat interior walls–easier to hang your art and pictures."There is a loft one flight up from the main floor."Five bedrooms, three full baths, wood and tile floors except bedrooms, Berber carpeted."Fully furnished by an expert professional design team–Tempur-Pedic beds."Is primitive-colonial in nature, with Shaker woodwork and cabinets, black custom wrought iron, brushed brass, and punched-tin treatments and hardware throughout."Complete entertainment centers include ninety-three-inch TV monitors and

Bose all-around media handlers in first-floor living space and in the daylight downstairs recreation area."A mightily designed desktop computer installed and placed at your desk in the office space. You'll also find a top-of-line laptop and a tablet or notebook there."Amber-stained and sealed exterior, hunter-green steel roof, black asphalt-paved driveway."All powered by natural gas, custom furnace and hot-water system; all appliances custom, best-of-breed brushed stainless steel."How are you so far, Richard?" Jake peers into Mack's eyes.

"Huh? Oh yeah…I'm keeping up. I like what I've heard so far. Thanks." Mack rubs his eyes.

"Central air and heat, but in case of a winter outage, you also have top-of-the-line Efel woodstoves—one in the upstairs dining area and another in the downstairs living area. Each season, you'll receive a cord of seasoned, split and stacked wood in each of your wood rings."There is an electric start generator outside near the back door. All you need to do is throw a switch on the circuit board and start up the ignition on the machine outside. It is powered by natural-substance synthetic pellets."Two vehicles: jacked Range Rover, Willys vintage edition, drab green; and a Mercedes S-Class, gloss dark blue."Here is your new phone. I've transferred your contacts and other data from your old phone. You have a private and incognito VPN cable connection supporting *all* device and media I/O."Here are your key rings: one for the home, one for the vehicles, one set extra for each right here."Here are all the financial hard copy you'll need, and I've been sliding over to you the manuals and others guides for all the aforementioned items—the washer and drier."

"Like every man actually reads the appliance manuals," says Mack.

"Finally, unless you have questions or comments, you'll find a booklet inside, a black three-ring binder on the dining table. The contents illustrate and provide directions to anything and anywhere you could ever possibly want to go. Feel free to explore."

"Wow. I mean, wow." Mack is impressed. "I think you've covered all the bases. Thank you."

"You're welcome, Richard," Jake concludes.

"We will deliver you to your new home in the early morning. We'll leave here this early evening," John says.

"What is the history of the land I just inherited?"

"It is the only residence in the middle of an 875-acre plot. You own it all. The home is crowned upon a small ledge hill on a 10-acre clearing. There will be no flooding worries. Ridley Lane was once a logging trail. You'll be living in a leveled old farming village from the mid-1800s.

"We hope you will find this comfortable and meets your every need. You have the associative numbers if you need anything at all. They are also in the binder I mentioned to you. You may put the rest of this stuff in your new attaché. Remember, you are now Dick Baldwin. Get used to it! If you use your former self's name, you do so at your own risk, and that is a deal breaker.

"Enjoy your life, Mr. Baldwin," Jake says then stands and walks out the door. Poof—just like that.

"Well, that was an abrupt departure," Mack says to John.

"He doesn't have time to around, I'd guess.

Hey, Mack, let's stay in touch. No reason we can't if we follow protocol. You already have a lifetime retainer with me as Richard Charles Baldwin."

No past.

—⚜ **25** ⚜—

In due time, Mack grows into an existence of happiness and wisely maintains his health in his Litchfield paradise. He accepts what is, what is not, and what can never be. He thrives on routine and his complete freedom, despite the restrictions under WitPro. But he slowly takes on learning how to make things happen for himself regardless of or within the program.

Making arrangements to see his son, daughter, and attorney, John is like disentangling a complex knot of rope then tying it up again. He steps into and out of situations with natural composure and dexterity. Without patting himself on the back, he realizes the progress he's made over time. Falling and staying asleep comes easy, even though his mornings come with difficulty. He accepts that too.

He takes dinner with Robin at least once a week; by default, usually over the weekends. The food comes from Robin's small farm garden with protein from the farm or hunted. Out here, there is no need for designated hunting seasons or licensing. Robin also grows a little cannabis, which they both enjoy after an ample, hearty dinner. These are welcomed times for both men, good times. Both guys are quite talkative over the low-volume music that perpetually plays in the background.

Hemp grows wild everywhere, but cannabis also in controlled areas, mostly over the outdated big-business tobacco farms.

Tobacco-production growth, processing, and packaging is outlawed for health reasons, but it's an import product still in use without consequence. Hemp is the major continental crop due in large part to Mack's activities that rise to the top of the sustainability tree of energy, as well as the law.

He is not a silent partner, although he teleconferences into meetings by proxy. No one knows or asks his name. He is the actor in the lead-architect role in the latest movement in fossil-fuel replacement. Everyone involved knows what he is, but not who he is.

Clear-cutting is tightly controlled and nearly obsolete. Tree harvesting must be in small rotating crops; and before a company is granted permission, it must pass a rigorous test of necessity, sustainability, and sensibility. Only where it must, trees are harvested and farmed rotationally, much like blueberries in New England.

Clothing, construction, and paper products are sourced in cotton, hemp, flax, or kenaf. After long activists' movements, flax, hemp, and algal-abundant fuels become a reality in the United States. Production and use of these renewable energy sources also spread, although slowly, across Europe and the East. Middle-Eastern countries are slow to convert for all the obvious reasons—money being the major blockade. Otherwise, Mack's ideas and the crusade behind them, socially and governmentally, globally take hold.

Costs come down after two years of the ideal refinement but then rest reasonably, just high enough so those in the new lines of business can make a decent and healthy living and set fair wages. Even though Mack refuses payment from the beginning, a meager yet steady $2.5 M dollars is direct deposited into his Fidelity account semiannually. The public is not aware, nor would they object, considering the contributions he's made, but salaries of all others in the relatively new business are disclosed. There are no complaints. There are no secrets, other than the country's—the new world's—hero.

Homes and businesses in the United States run entirely on wind, hydro, and solar power. It is Mack's and the enterprise program's wish, plan, and push to convert energy sourcing all over the world. On this front, there is virtually no pushback. Some areas more than others use more or less of any one of the resources depending on location, climate, and ready availability. It is not in the enterprise's aim to force any territory to spend exorbitant amounts of money to take the ideas forward. Mack's designees manage and account for the international budget like the NFL—all the countries share their earnings and savings with one another. Equality is the goal.

An excerpt from the mission statement includes "All countries for all."

Low budgeting on the road to conversion to clean energy is in writing, also part of the program strategy mission statement. No one is interested in breaking anyone else. The early-on activists calling for this kind of change—their children and their children as well—find themselves in a world they prayed for, marched for, and stood up for so many years, lifetimes. It takes over forty years for this definitive change to occur, but finally—*it does*.

Ladies, gentlemen, and young people of all ages, it is accepted, dress and groom with no accordance but in the ways they contribute to the solution, such as keeping the new mills open and up and running and to keep people working. The movement is persistently creating jobs. Over the half decade in the USA alone, the enterprise is responsible for the creation of many hundreds of thousands of jobs, approaching the millions.

High society takes on a whole new meaning, but not in the negative sense fought against by the conservatives of the past. Folks work at a production rate of every person easily exerting the throughput of two. GDP is way up. People have a focus not seen since the 1990s. Labeling "stoners" is a thing of the past. Dress doesn't matter. Hair doesn't either. Technology is finally catching up with spirituality.

Some work high; some do not. Whatever works best for them and their employers is what matters. Managers everywhere still conduct periodic evaluations and appraisals, no different than ever before, except that the ratings assignment is obliterated. No one is associated with a code, number, or textual flag. Simple guidelines are set, and managers are encouraged to employ methodologies that work the best for them and, more importantly, their staff.

❦ **26** ❦

"My, how times evolve, huh, Robin?"

"I'm not out there, but I read enough and hear enough from you to know," Robin replies to Mack.

"When I was a very young information scientist, things were much, much different," Mack says.

"Oh, I could imagine. You know how my work history looks. How things were for me. I really admire you, man."

"Yes, Robin, I do. That's partially why I invited you here. And thank you."

"Best move I ever made!" Robin laughs.

With a chuckle, Mack says, "Well, I'm glad you're here, brother."

Chuck briefs Mack monthly on the legal process generated by the Advanced Energy reports, testimony, and other statements provided. Unbelievably long tentacles stretch from the Department of Justice outward. The only continent untouched and kept at bay is Russia. They are not involved in the crimes and don't need to know any more than the public at large. Mack is amazed. He had no idea of the network of crooks in the dialogue over Advanced Energy from the relatively short list of project sponsors he knows and submitted.

Perhaps currently moot by virtue of Mack's monumental resolution, a comparison early on of Carbon Tax with Emissions Trading sparks. The discussion about climate change centers on federal legislation to reduce fossil fuel emissions. The major options for widespread reductions are a carbon tax and cap-and-trade of emissions.

In cap-and-trade, the government sets a limit on the allowable amount of emissions coughed out. Over time, the government hypothetically reduces that limit. The purchases made by polluters in an emissions market that deals with permits to pollute are referred to as trades. In essence, the buyers are fined for polluting.

With the carbon tax, the government levies a pollution fee on the first sale of a fossil fuel after extraction or import. This upstream taxation applies to relatively few providers of fossil fuels, simplifying the administration. The added cost flows down to retail consumers, motivating reduction in usage.

The way Mack understands it, the carbon tax is more effective than cap-and-trade because the simpler tax is easier to enforce and can be raised periodically to motivate further reductions in fossil fuel usage. In other words, if usage is not decreasing fast enough to meet goals for reductions, the Environmental Protection Agency raises the tax. Simple enough: to increase political acceptance of the new tax, the proceeds would fund an associated dividend that returns the tax revenues to the American people.

As the tax increases over the years to meet emissions reduction goals, the dividend increases. But the revenues are rarely delivered, and both practices put inordinate amounts of power, funds, and control in the government, big business, and Wall Street. No surprise there.

To build a broad base of support for continued increases, the dividends are theoretically distributed in equal amounts to all Americans, especially benefiting lower income groups who in general use less fuel. Consumers who reduce their carbon tax expense through energy conservation and through buying energy from renewable sources realize more of a benefit. And this much does appear suppositionally to be true. This financial benefit provides strong and effective motivation to reduce fossil fuel usage. But Mack wants to know how the poor and needy are supposed to afford to install and purchase these new energy-efficient appliances? He seems to find one loose end after another hanging off both incentives.

The tax, it is said by Congress, increases

the value of projects to install renewable energy sources by increasing the cost of fossil fuels. The tax also makes renewables easier to invest in because returns on the investments can be estimated more accurately than under cap-and-trade with its speculative emissions trading, increasing the variability of energy cost.

On paper, it suggests that there are decent intentions documented. So, renewables are on our minds, even if the money flows into the effort, the baseline knowledge and know-how is missing. And these governmental counterfeit and sham solutions remain stalled after decades of hide-and-seek. That void is open for Mack to fill, and it is indeed a vacuum.

This is how he sees things: Cap-and-trade is less effective because polluters trade away the responsibility to reduce emissions at the source. The probability of abuse of the wide-ranging, complex emissions-trading system implies that the goals for emissions reduction would not be met after accounting for fraudulent permits and inaccurately measured emissions.

If cap-and-trade underperformed, it would be difficult to abandon the system because of entrenched beneficiaries such as traders, brokers, financiers, attorneys, and an extensive and expensive new regulatory bureaucracy. The income derived by those beneficiaries of cap-and-trade would add substantially to the costs of energy and of government. Mack's short rebuttal:

Many capped businesses would devote significant effort to trying to utilize the system to continue business as usual instead of reducing emissions. Rather than wasting that effort on the distraction of cap-and-trade, the carbon tax would motivate businesses to focus on actually reducing usage of fossil fuels.

The truth is that offsets are sold into the emissions market associated with cap-and-trade. They pose persistent problems of quantification and verification of carbon dioxide absorbed. Beyond fundamental problems with barely sincere attempts to quantify offsets, often the value is substantially overstated by fraudulent application of the offset's cumulative effects over its entire extended lifetime against present-day emissions.

A well-known but flawed offset tries to compensate for the heat-trapping emissions from personal travel by funding the planting of trees. Certainly, it's desirable to donate money for tree planting. However, Mack reasons, when planting is used as an offset, counterproductive effects occur. The extra blankets from the present-day emissions supposedly compensated by the offset remain over the earth. Those extra blankets cause warming during the growth of the trees for decades. Therefore, the usage of tree planting as an offset ironically *builds in* warming during those decades.

In the cycle, emissions from decomposing organic matter get absorbed during photosynthesis and by other means. Burning fossil fuels adds human-induced carbon to the natural cycle. No known financially feasible offset removes carbon from the cycle.

For people planning to sell offsets, the value would probably be undercut by competition from inexpensive offsets from abroad. Such offsets would worsen the balance of trade.

The simple truth, Mack easily understands, is that offsets do not correct emissions at the source. Polluters purchase the offsets to continue business as usual. Meritorious projects must be funded by other means than offsets.

Considering the problems with corruption plaguing many governments, cap-and-trade is problematic with its many difficult-to-verify transactions. The transparent nature of the carbon tax, while not entirely a positive gesture, makes it more readily applicable.

A carbon tax delivers revenue to a nation's government rather than to private entities, motivating the government to enforce compliance. Each government maintains national sovereignty, arriving at its own balance between returning the tax revenues to citizens and investing in energy efficiency and renewables.

Mack creates a graph and narrative using China as a working example. He documents the illustration: "The tax would be more competent especially in the case of China because strict caps would *not* be feasible there. China has decentralized so that provincial governments make their own decisions about energy generation. Those governments see continued economic growth as essential to their survival because hundreds of millions of subsistence farmers expect to rise out of poverty. If the central Chinese government attempted to enforce meaningful caps on provincial governments, they probably would reject them firmly.

"However, with a US carbon tax, a border tax adjustment could be made to equalize tax expense between taxing and nontaxing states and territories. That adjustment could influence provincial governments in China to support a Chinese carbon tax because of the effect of the US adjustment on their competitiveness and growth.

"Moreover, the central government of China probably would succeed in imposing a national carbon tax because it would not set up a fierce internal battle with and among the provincial governments as might setting caps region by region. After all, corporation taxes have long been collected nationwide in China, and the personal income tax has recently been initiated."Mack is satisfied that the report he's reading and his documented interpretations are strong and accurate.

Concern has been expressed about damaging America's international competitiveness if strong federal legislation got enacted. The utility of a border tax adjustment could allay that concern, easing passage in the United States of the legislation for a carbon tax.

Under cap-and-trade, an adjustment would not be effective. In international terms, a cap is a quota that restrains trade, so that Mack's argument is made that the adjustment would be equivalent to imposing quotas. The World Trade Organization's General Agreement on Tariffs and Trade does not allow quotas, setting the stage for cap-and-trade's adjustment to be contested in a dispute lasting for years. If ultimately, the adjustment were defeated, as seems likely, year after year, the world would still be without a protocol for reducing emissions of fossil fuels.

Mack simplifies:

"Therefore, cap-and-trade would not be useful for effecting the necessary long-term reductions worldwide. In contrast, the simpler carbon tax could be implemented worldwide in a relatively short time.

"The first step for those concerned to take is to sign the petition introduced by the Price Carbon Organization. Beyond promoting the carbon tax and dividend in Washington, citizens have the opportunity to promote it nationwide among the leaders of the grassroots, especially local elected officials."Mack's promotion does away with the problems introduced by the American government and around the globe. He makes an effort to make existing iterations of carbon tax ideals work, make sense. As his project takes flight, he plans to explain away the current, failing quick fixes.

Actions are the mission of the parent Federal Carbon Tax Organization, which makes available as a public service a sample resolution in support of the federal tax for city, town, or county governments to consider. Surprisingly, no monetary donation is solicited. An action plan for working with local officials details how any citizen, elected or not, can help get the resolution introduced. A sample letter to an official is available.

Once the resolution is passed by the local government, it sends copies of the resolution to officials representing the government at the national level, signaling that a federal carbon tax could become politically possible. The resolution requires no further commitment on the part of the local government. Officials inform their constituents of the advantages of the tax when they explain their votes. Local media coverage of the passage amplifies the message. Again, a government going over the shoulder to get back to the pinky.

The time from contacting an official to passage can be as little as three months. Within a year, dozens of resolutions could be passed nationwide, informing the people and letting Washington know that common sense can prevail.

Hmmm, so where are these public notices from their officials in DC?

Following this feasible method, supposedly, as more local governments pass such resolutions, the increasing magnitude of the news could inspire the introduction of more resolutions, bringing greater nationwide attention to the advantages of the tax and dividend, and building momentum for a mandate.

Some officials object that local governance needs to emphasize local issues. However, in a democracy, we the people also need to pay some attention to broader issues that impact citizens at both the local and the national levels.

So, in conclusion over the subject, Mack documents:

"At stake is earth as our nurturing mother.

"Let's not put the earth-critical process

of reducing emissions into the hands of traders and financiers who are pitching deals. Let us get this epochal, overarching environmental policy decision right, enacting the more effective, economical, equitable, and timely carbon tax, not built-broken cap-and-auction, a boondoggle with many linkages for failure. Just in the meantime.

"Better yet, redesign and accelerate our steps with our attention paid to the King Biomass and Planet Fix Reports."**27**

The United States Department of Energy, also known as the DOE, is a cabinet-level department of the United States government concerned with the United States' policies regarding energy and safety in handling nuclear material. They represent the bulk of defendants in the Advanced Energy case. Its responsibilities include the nation's nuclear weapons program, nuclear reactor production for the United States Navy, energy conservation, energy-related research, radioactive waste disposal, and domestic energy production. It also directs research in genomics: the Human Genome Project originated in a DOE initiative. DOE sponsors more research in the physical sciences than any other US federal agency, the majority of which is conducted through its system of national laboratories.

In 1974, the Atomic Energy Commission gave way to the Nuclear Regulatory Commission, which was tasked with regulating the nuclear power industry, and the Energy Research and Development Administration, which was tasked to manage the nuclear weapon, naval reactor, and energy development programs.

The 1973 oil crisis called attention to the need to consolidate energy policy. In 1977, the US president signed into law The Department of Energy Organization Act of

1977, which created the Department of Energy. The new agency, which began operations in late 1977, consolidated the Federal Energy Administration, the Energy Research and Development Administration, the Federal Power Commission, and programs of various other agencies.

The department is under the control and supervision of the United States secretary of Energy, a political appointee of the president of the United States. The Energy secretary is assisted in managing the department by a United States deputy secretary of Energy, also appointed by the president, who assumes the duties of the secretary in his absence.

The department also has three undersecretaries, each appointed by the president, who oversee the major areas of the department's work. The president also appoints seven officials with the rank of assistant secretary of Energy who have line management responsibility for major organizational elements of the department. The Energy secretary assigns their functions and duties. With news of Advanced Energy arrests and investigations, they and other higher-up hand in their resignations.

The extensive defendants in the Advanced Energy trial within this cabinet are the secretary of Energy, deputy secretary, undersecretary for Science and Energy, assistant secretary for Fossil Energy, assistant secretary for Energy Efficiency and Renewable Energy, assistant secretary for Nuclear Energy, assistant secretary for Electricity Delivery and Energy Reliability, general counsel, chief financial officer, enterprise assessments, Energy policy and system analysis, and the intelligence and counterintelligence.

It is proven that they all played a part in funding, sponsoring or were stakeholders in the corrupt Advanced Energy effort.

As a leading federal research and development agency in the United States, the Department of Energy operates a system of national laboratories and technical facilities. Under the incursion of the international crimes brought against them, the DOE national laboratories are subpoenaed, including Ames Laboratory, Argonne National Laboratory, Brookhaven National Laboratory, Fermi National Accelerator Laboratory, Idaho National Laboratory, Lawrence Berkeley National Laboratory, Lawrence Livermore National Laboratory, Los Alamos National Laboratory, National Energy Technology Laboratory, National Renewable Energy Laboratory, Oak

Ridge National Laboratory, Pacific Northwest National Laboratory, Princeton Plasma Physics Laboratory, Sandia National Laboratories, Savannah River National Laboratory, and the Thomas Jefferson National Accelerator Facility.

The other major DOE facilities under scrutiny include Albany Research Center, National Petroleum Technology Office, Office of Fossil Energy, Radiological and the Environmental Sciences Laboratory. All of these legally targeted individuals and groups came together with the interrogation of just seven of the sixteen official Advanced Energy project sponsors.

Almost all these defendants are looking at doing lengthy time and paying hefty fines. Some claim the Fifth Amendment.

The president unveils in early 2024 a $26.4 billion budget request for DOE for fiscal year 2025, including $12.3 billion for the DOE Office of Energy Efficiency and Renewable Energy. The budget aims to substantially expand the use of renewable energy sources while improving energy transmission infrastructure. It also makes significant investments in hybrids and plug-in hybrids, in smart grid technologies, and in scientific research and innovation. Those acts implicate even the office of the president of the United States, which is unknowingly under a microscope.

As part of the $789 billion economic stimulus package in the American Recovery and Reinvestment Act II of 2025, Congress provides Energy with an additional $38.3 billion for fiscal years 2026 and 2027, adding about 75 percent to Energy's annual budgets.

Most of the stimulus spending was in the form of grants and contracts.

Energy savings performance contracts are contracts under which a contractor designs, constructs, and obtains the necessary financing for an energy savings project, and the federal agency makes payments over time to the contractor from the savings in the agency's utility bills. The contractor guarantees the energy improvements will generate savings, and after the contract ends, all continuing cost savings accrue to the federal agency.

Contractual members and committee chairpersons are under investigation.

Energy innovation hubs are multidisciplinary, meant to advance highly promising areas of energy science and technology from their early stages of research to the point that the risk level will be low enough for industry to commercialize the technologies. The Consortium for Advanced Simulation of Light Water Reactors was the first DOE energy innovation hub established in July 2020, for the purpose of providing advanced modeling and simulation solutions for commercial nuclear reactors.

Mack builds in a transparent transfer of DOE and other funds to the Biomass Energy project. The DOE budget includes $280 million to fund eight energy innovation hubs, each of which will focus on a particular energy challenge.

Two of the eight hubs dispersed within various budgets and focused on integrating smart materials, designs, and systems into buildings to better conserve energy and on designing and discovering new concepts and materials needed to convert solar energy into electricity.

Another two hubs included in the DOE Office of Science budget will tackle the challenges of devising advanced methods of energy storage and creating fuels directly from sunlight without the use of plants or microbes. Yet another hub will develop smart materials that will allow the electrical grid to adapt and respond to changing conditions. In an easy lateral shift of attention, Mack's reports' projects secure human and monetary resources by contract and does so immensely.

Even the official seal of the Department of Energy is not overlooked. It includes a green shield bisected by a gold-colored lightning bolt, on which is emblazoned a gold-colored symbolic sun, atom, oil derrick, windmill, and dynamo. It is crested by the white head of an eagle atop a white rope. Both appear on a blue field surrounded by concentric circles in which the name of the agency, in gold, appears on a green background. Mack intends to petition for a change to the seal that excludes the oil derrick upon completion of his proposals and projects.

$$\text{---} \otimes\text{ } \textbf{28}\text{ } \otimes \text{---}$$

Mack keeps up with and submits follow-up plans for Biomass Energy, as he refers to the efforts as an ongoing project. An easy, understandable, and pointed title. The United States, under the direction of Mack and his solutions, establish plantations cleverly across the nation to maintain growth of hemp, cotton, flax and kenaf. Hatcheries and new installations include or are dedicated to algae for algal abundant fuel production.

Kenaf is a warm-season annual fiber crop closely related to cotton and okra that can be successfully produced in a large portion of the United States, particularly in the southern states. Kenaf farms are established alongside most of the existing cotton crops. Additional cotton and kenaf fields come as a deliverable of Biomass Energy.

As the commercial use of kenaf continues to diversify from its historical role as a cordage crop to its various new applications including paper products, building materials, absorbents, renewable fuel, and livestock feed, choices within the decision matrix continue to increase and involve issues ranging from basic agricultural production methods to marketing of kenaf products. These management decisions require an understanding of the many different facets of kenaf production as a fiber, feed, and seed crop.

For productive hemp farming, deep humus-rich, nutrient-rich soil with controlled water flow is preferable. Water-logged acidic, compressed, or extremely light or sandy soils primarily affect the early development of plants. Crop evaluators avoid steep and high altitudes of more than three hundred miles above sea level. Hemp is relatively insensitive to cold temperatures and can withstand frost down to negative five degrees. Water requirement of hemp is at least fourteen times lower than that of cotton.

Hemp benefits crops grown after it. For this reason, it is grown before winter cereals. Advantageous changes are high weed suppression, soil loosening by the large hemp root system, and the positive effect on soil tilth. Since hemp is very self-compatible, it can also be grown several years in a row in the same fields.

Hemp farms are kept separated from the cannabis strains that also grow fluently as most regulations are dropped and rewritten for the benefit of the farmers as well as the users. Cannabis replaces tobacco, which is now an import in fair trade agreements branching out to several countries. Cannabis fields exist across the top third of the nation and some in the South—inside and out.

Flax tolerates a range of soils and climates and can be grown in almost any part of the United States. Sites in full sun, with deep, fertile, well-drained soil are sought and developed. Farmers prepare it as if it were for growing vegetables or flowers. Flax grows best in cool weather, so it is sown outdoors as soon as the soil can be worked in spring at the same time as other cool-weather crops.

AFTERWORD

Avengers hired on and devoted to Advanced Energy report to Al Kahtani as they continue their search for Mack and others. They do not have the means by which to find him, or anyone for that matter, enrolled in the Witness Protection Program. No one does and never has. That Mack is able to see his ideas come to materialization, actualization all from his hideaway is awe-inspiring. His secrets, his past are buried forever.

Those who wish him harm do not waver. They know it is likely that Mack is in WitPro, so they do all they can to spot activity with anyone and everyone who may be or were ever a part of Mack's life. No luck yet locating his children. Basic elements of WitPro include safeguard, security, and stability of familial ties. Mack is a widower, and he lost touch with the few family members he may have ever been close with at all, which would go all the way back to young childhood. His children, however, are given WitPro treatment for their own safety and well-being.

His son, Beacon, is relocating from New Jersey to Connecticut and given a new identity: Journey Samuel Gallagher. He and younger sister, Ailis, understand fully as they were early on given an opportunity to spend a week with Mack at his place in Litchfield. Mack's daughter, Ailis, requests that she be relocated to Maine, not far from her dad. She is pleased with her new name: Alia Karis Gallagher.

The US marshal who delivers the children to their father spends a full day with the King's to explain in full, for the sake of the young adults, how the program works.

"The United States Witness Protection Program is one that is seen a lot in movies and on television. But in these instances, the audience is only seeing the basics and may think that it's simply a matter of the witness testifying and then moving to another location under a new name and new identity." The marshal begins and then continues to explain that although these are in fact the basics of Witness Protection, there is much more to this program than simply packing up and leaving.

"It involves much more than simply moving one person to another location. Their old identities need to be stricken from all records; new identities need to be set in place, established; and new lives need to be given to them. We've completed the process for your father and are nearly finished with plans for you two."

"Am I going to be in Maine?" Ailis asks, "near my dad?"

"We are pleased to be able to do that for you."

She smiles as wide as Mack has ever seen, which pleases him.

"Here is some introductory info for you. Just bear with me here. These people are now among your best friends: there are three different federal organizations that are involved in placing an eligible person into the Witness Protection Program, and they each focus on particular areas within the program. I won't bore you with the details, but these organizations and their areas of responsibility are the United States Marshals Service. We ensure that the participants who don't go to jail are kept safe, secure, and healthy."The US Department of Justice, Office of Enforcement Operations. This organization determines who is allowed to be placed into the program."Federal Bureau of Prisons. This organization oversees the incarceration of those deemed guilty after conviction."

"Yeah," Beacan says. "But how do we disappear? I mean…really."

"Okay, guys. The entry process and having your identity completely erased, here we go.

"Once a person has been deemed in need of the Witness Protection program, the Marshals Service will then go about trying to make that person 'fall off the face of the earth.' This includes things such as creating a new identity for the subject and his family as well as finding somewhere that they may be relocated.

"But creating the new identity is not done by the Marshals Service alone. It involves many different government agencies and top secrecy. Some may think that assuming a new identity will give them a clean slate when it comes to things such as loans and outstanding debts as the creditors will now no longer be able to find the witness. However, these and any other necessary obligations must be met before the person will be placed into Witness Protection."

"No worries kids," Mack says. "I've got all three of us covered. And I'll help set you up to get started."

"Once the witness has met with the Marshals Service," the US marshal continues, "they and their family, and any other endangered persons related to the case, will be taken from their current location right away and will be moved to another location. This is not, however, their new home. It is simply a temporary location where they will remain safe prior to their move.

"You will indeed be able to begin a new life for yourselves once in the new permanent location. However, the reason for you being there will not be a complete secret from everyone. The Marshals Service will tell the local law enforcement agency what you are doing in the new location and will reveal all details of any past criminal activity. You two have none.

"However, the Marshals Service will also help you adjust to life in your new community as well as they can. They may or may not find a reasonable job opportunity for you, help you find a place to live, provide you with funds for living, approximately $60,000 a year."

"Take advantage of that, kids. Sorry to interrupt, sir."

"Okay, next, we give you, and anyone else who has taken on an assumed identity, proper identification documentation, make arrangements for any necessary counselling.

"For the first short little while that you are in witness protection, the Marshals Service will also provide twenty-four-hour security, especially when the situation is high-risk."

"So where is our temporary place, Marshal?" Beacan asks.

"We are there. Your dad is secured here now, so this is it."

"Why didn't you tell us?" Ailis asks a bit perturbed.

"We want to make certain that a secret is a secret. It is not a matter of trust. It is a matter of the best way to handle our responsibilities, your safety. We think this arrangement is a perfect opportunity that fell right into our laps. Seems like a no-brainer. That's all."

"So what happens after the relocation?" Beacan wants to know.

"All right. Let's see if I can get all this in nice and clear for you. Once you have been moved to your new location, you must *never* return to the location that you left. You also must *never* contact any family members or friends who are not protected. I would encourage you also to aggressively pursue employment opportunities and new friends. If you should fail to do so, all payments from the government will automatically be stopped.

However, the protected can apply for government assistance should they wish to do so.

"According to the Marshals Service, no witness or related family who has kept to the rules has ever been found, injured, or killed by the parties that they testified against. After you have settled into your new life, you must still contact the government officials once a year, but this is much less than the contact that is required while you are adjusting to your new life. However, you must always contact the government should you choose to move. If anyone wishes to contact you after you've relocated, they can only do so once they have made a request to the Marshals Service." The marshal takes a deep breath, smiles, and looks around the living room at everyone.

Mack is looking at his children. The kids

are staring nose down at their hands between their knees. The two older men leave them to their thoughts but remain peeked to answer any questions that may come up. Mack is pretty sure his daughter will have plenty; his son, some.

"Dad," Beacan says with tears streaming down his face, "I want to tell you…You are a hero out there, you know. Everywhere. You are the most famous folklore-like savior ever in the world. I'm like trying to understand everything you have done and are doing. I am really proud of you…to be your son." He steps over to Mack and hugs him, holding tight and long.

Mack's eyes are full of tears. They softly spill over and run down his cheeks. "I love you, Beacon."

"It's true, Dad," Ailis adds excitedly. "You

are like the most admired person ever! I am in awe."

Mack still feels weepy as he gets up and gathers his children into his arms and hugs them tightly.

"Kids, thank you for telling me that," Mack says with a cracked voice. "But what I did and what I am doing now is not for notoriety. It is for the good of all man and the planet."

Mack is up and running on dark bold coffee and does what he does first every morning: he checks his e-mail. There is a new message requesting help with recovery operations from the damage caused by Advanced Energy. The cleanup team leader also asks him how to dismantle the makeshift underwater rigs that Advanced Energy planted.

Mack downloads an oceanographic map of the Atlantic seafloor. Using a photo editor, he creates a new layer as he carefully draws a red line that represents the location of the fault created by Advanced Energy. He creates another layer, and following along the red line on the layer beneath, he marks with a small bold black *x* every site Advanced Energy pulverized.

Mack uses traditional degrees within longitude and latitude in his narrative that accompanies the oceanographic map. He draws a legend in the bottom right corner that, in simple terms, specify that the red channel represents the fault line that must be forced closed. That should happen after the apparatus is removed. He footnotes that his instructions in how to do so follow. He specifies that the recovery team will find the resource guzzling apparatus at each location marked. He adds another note stating that the details on how to disassemble each rig follow.

Finally, on a separate map, he gives the Unites States' east coast the same treatment, indicating likely locations of Advanced Energy Phase II operations to date. He makes it clear that in this case, his designations are somewhat speculative, though likely. The point is that the operations hardware is out there.

Decommissioning and dismantling projects underwater take capabilities that extend to include project management, technical support, manpower, and special equipment beyond what they originally plan. The combination of extensive equipment resources and a multi-skilled workforce is necessary to bring the added value everyone wants and what the world needs throughout the decommissioning process.

Mack conceives a repeatable process, which he draws as a system flow and narrates in pseudo-technical grammar. Given the support vessels and robotics, the first thing to do is recover the full bladder of resource. The second thing to do is to plant small, tightly controlled, and slackened demolition encasements in and along targeted key positions all around and in the rig.

Once that is complete, the third task is to build an all-encompassing enclosure that encases, blocks off, and hems in the entire underwater rig. Then detonations take place that turn the custom rigs to a box of loose scrap metal and other material. A recognizance vessel, such as a sea barge or a large container or cargo ship above slowly reels up the enclosed box of waste: the demolished rig.

While that action takes place, a custom ROV

cuts the pipe at the floor and fills it with sealant and cement. An alternate approach would be to use a high-powered pulley to yank the entire length of pipe out of the spot. Either way, the feed shaft must be immediately closed, sealed. And Mack refers to the part of this document that speaks to closing the fault line.

Mack's instructions on how to close the linear crack in the nadir begin by pointing out the fundamental and essential machinery and accessories. The project includes remotely operated robotic vehicles (ROVs) specially equipped with attachments, such as backhoes, bulldozers, and stabilizing spurs and jets. They must be able to withstand any current encountered along the widened line.

The operation is restricted to adjust only the man-made fault line platelets and not the natural faults, such as the Atlantic's triple junction of the Eurasian Plate, North American Plate, and the African Plate. Mack suggests the progress move from north to south because the indicative danger is more critical in its coming than in the south.

The backhoe pulls layers of platelets inward from both sides, then the bulldozer pushes and forces them together from each side inward. Mack theorizes that the pressure of ocean waters above help hold the platelets in place. The water may cause further movement, but not a pull: more a push that will have better settled the plates into place.

Biomass Energy is leading the way before cutting through the trial that is finally nearing the end, and consulting on what he calls Planet Fix, the name of his new S Corp formed in Delaware. Mack has no trouble juggling his responsibilities and efforts. With his manic tendencies, his energy level is generally high. He does long for the day when all he has to commit himself to is Biomass Energy, furthermore, Planet Fix, and whatever may come afterward.

And globalization is what that is. He is confident that with closer guidance, instruction, and general cheerleading, the Biomass Energy movement will spread inconsequentially and indefinitely. The overall vision is one where every territory everywhere is on sustainability, sustenance, and renewables, with the exception of the central Middle Eastern countries. But he vows he'll never let up or give up on those peoples. But sadly, freedom, liberty, and human rights are yet to be reality there.

The Big Five oil companies begin to limit exploration around 2026. The international oil companies are spending less money on oil exploration in real terms despite a fourfold increase in operating cash flow since the early-2020s. On the flip side, numerous studies find that second-tier oil companies are spending more in exploration, positioning themselves to be in better shape when it comes to future oil reserves.

The studies find that the Big Five used 66 percent of their increasing cash flow on share repurchases and dividends, which were good for investors in the short-term but put at risk company long-term oil reserves.

"The prognostication is on the wall: the foretaste is on our plates. The oil majors are not replacing reserves," testifies Mary Anne Jeffers, coauthor of one of the reports and fellow for Energy Studies at the Randal Institute.

"It's as if they are slowly liquidating their long-term asset base. They may see a declining rate of production over time, and eventually, that is bad news for both their shareholders and consumers.

"State-owned monopolies, known as national oil companies represent the top ten oil reserve holders internationally. By comparison, the Big Five are ranked thirteenth, fourteenth, seventeenth, nineteenth, and twenty-fifth. They still rank among the largest oil and gas producers worldwide, and these Western majors have also achieved a dramatically higher return on capital than national oil companies of similar size.

"The Big Five are still an important force in the market. Their production represents over twenty percent of non-OPEC production," adds Jeffers.

"But investors are placing a higher premium for the stock shares of emerging national oil companies, despite the measurable edge the majors have in terms of operational efficiency. Clearly, they are betting on who will own the oil in the future. Last week's announcement that Brazil's state oil company had an eight-billion-barrel discovery is a case in point."

"Thank you very much, Ms. Jeffers."

A portion of the prosecution's closing arguments include a study findings summary:

"Exploration spending of the five international oil companies or IOCs has been flat or lower in the aftermath of OPEC's reinvigorated effort to constrain market supply in 2018. Given the uptick in costs of material, personnel, and equipment, such as drilling rigs, the five largest have cut spending levels in real terms over the past ten years. This trend appears, however, to be easing, with exploration spending, by the five increasing IOCs rising by fifty percent in 2026 over 2023.

"Instead of favoring exploration, the five largest IOCs used 66 percent of their increased operating cash flow in 2026 on share repurchases and dividends. They have also increased spending on developed resources, presumably to monetize these assets quickly while oil prices are high.

"The next twenty largest privately traded US oil firms have not followed a similar pattern. Instead, they have steadily increased exploration spending since 2016, and their spending now equals that of the five largest IOCs. This differing pattern comes despite the fact that the five largest IOCs have access to operating cash flow that is three times the size of the next twenty largely traded American oil firms. This trend indicates that these twenty next-largest privately traded American firms will control an increasing portion of non-OPEC oil production in the coming years.

"Oil production of the five largest oil companies has, on paper, declined since the mid-2010s. Oil production for the five largest IOCs fell from 10.25 million barrels a day in 2023 to 9.45 million in 2025 before rebounding to 9.7 million barrels a day in 2026. By contrast, for the next twenty US independent oil firms, their oil production has risen since 2026, from 1.55 million barrels a day in 2016 to about 2.13 million in 2025 and 2026.

"What this displays is where a wealth of missing funds goes. Ladies and gentlemen, they're going to Advanced Energy. You heard from a dozen industry experts and witnesses before Ms. Jeffers. You've heard the eye witness testimony from three dozen men and women who were lured into Advanced Energy under false pretenses. It is clear that the Big Five IOCs and some other independent firms clearly conspired and poured monies into the secret resource, finding expedition and illegal sourcing that is Advanced Energy. May I offer under even the president of the United States' watch.

"There is no innocent subject, not one at that defense's table.

Thank you."

Joan Dempsey secures an attorney, and after some talk, he agrees to let her offer an official affidavit—her report for 100

percent immunity. Her attorney guarantees interrogators that she probably knows more of the Advanced Energy details than anyone else they have, except perhaps Mackenzie King.

Joan knows well all those who have yet to be questioned, including the entire support staff at the Sleepy Hollow lab, such as the security force put in place, the envoys and other fringe individuals, valets, drivers and chauffeurs. Joan names names, offers dates, and because she was the attending scribe in almost every meeting, she hands over the journal she kept containing copies of plans, quotes, statements, and incriminating artifacts—the entirety of her scribe's notes— among other official classified documentation, in exchange for immunity.

She testifies for the state and feds via teleconference, disguised—much like the handling of Mack. Her testimony forges that, relative of Mack's into place, virtually undeniable. The judge orders subpoenas for search and seizure over all the new actors introduced by Joan.

She is advised to go into the WitPro program. Joan takes that advice, and her attorney notifies the US Marshals. She can't stand any of the bits of family she has left, and she has no real, true, honest friends anymore. They all seemed to miss maturation. So the program, as it is described to her, sounds more like a reward to her than it does a depravity. They send her to Fort Lauderdale, Florida.

The witnesses from the staff at Sleepy Hollow can only concur with portions of previous statements of others. They are worth hearing from even though they do not add anything new. It is clear that it is just a job for them. Most are either Spanish or are Muslims just trying to support their families. They have no idea that anything underhanded is going on.

As soon as she is dismissed by Al Kahtani, Charlie returns to her home in the south of France. When she learns of the Whistle Reports and the trial following, she retains her lawyer. They sit together in his office, where Charlie talks through the entire operation. She maintains that she has no idea that Advanced Energy is not a well-founded and legitimate effort for certain appropriate, genuine, and lawful sponsors.

In the meantime, her attorney suggests she go into hiding until the trial is over with. She moves in with a close friend of hers who lives privately in a hideaway near the shore. The attorney agrees that he or they should keep an eye out for any news about Al Kahtani. He is on the loose and intends to kill everyone involved with the project who might implicate him. Charlie spends a full afternoon with her lawyer who brings her up to date on all things Advanced Energy. She knows about King: he is a hero. She knows about all the other players who live through it and those who do not.

Upon dismissal from Advanced Energy, Omar El Mofty easily slips back into Saudi Arabia. As usual, he travels under false identification. He is a man in demand and has another project within two weeks. He reports to that job in Nigeria and is settled into his pace almost immediately. Advanced Energy is a contracted distant past effort—no more, no less.

Just before their appearances in court, Hall and Cooper change their addresses and run with their families. Hall moves from Texas to Lafayette, Louisiana. Cooper relocates from Harbor Country, Michigan to Cleveland, Ohio. Al Kahtani's scouts report the locations as soon as they are found.

Sanjay Ganesh and Isaak Al Kahtani are on the run and in hiding with a small group of bad men, scouts. Kahtani directs searches for and then contracts Ganesh and the group to coordinate the murder of the team managers. Ganesh carries out the assassinations of Hall and Cooper. A quick cap to the back of the head is all it takes.

King is MIA and that is driving Al Kahtani nuts. Ganesh does not like Al Kahtani's neurotic behavior: it scares him. Ganesh wakes in the middle of the night and begins to get ready. He is bringing only a carry-on duffle bag. Just as Ganesh reaches for the exit door, Al Kahtani stabs him in the neck.

As Ganesh crouches on the floor, gurgling and gargling with each breath, Kahtani kicks him over. Al Kahtani quickly drags the still blood-bubbling Ganesh into an unused room and shoots him, killing Ganesh as he attempts an escape back to India.

Al Kahtani receives a tip from the only informer he has as on the prosecution, which keeps him and his hitmen interested as they continue the search for King. Using the traitor's information, they get dangerously close to Mack's daughter.

A US marshal alerts Mack. He confides in Robin. Robin insists Mack turn him loose on Al Kahtani. But Mack has another idea. Robin is a dark horse. He has deep and broad street smarts. No one knows him. No one knows where he resides. He knows how to do this. He stakes out at Alia's, and as soon as the watchers arrive, he notifies Mack. And Mack calls upon Fred.

"Fred," Mack begins. "It's Mack."

"Holy shit, Mack! How ya doin'?"

"Can we talk? Is your phone secured with scramble?"

"Yes," Fred says. "Of course it is. What's up, buddy?"

"Not good, brother. I need the angels, man."

"Okay, okay, what's up?"

"There are bad, bad people closing in on my daughter in Lewiston."

"So what are you thinkin'?

"I have a watcher very near her place: He knows what to look for. When he sees him or them, he will call me, and then I would call you."

"Well, first let me think over your plan. I might be able to do you one better."

"Well, I was trying not to take up too much of your guys' time—"

"Nonsense! Give me the afternoon, and I'll call you back.

By the way, what do you want done to the guy or guys once we have 'em?"

"I'd like them followed to their hideout and then killed. All of them. There ain't a decent man in the bunch. How you handle it is up to you, of course."

"Heavy shit, Mack—"

"I know. I know."

"Hey, hey, no problem, right? Okay? We've got this. Okay, man?"

"Yeah. Yes. Thank you so much, Fred. This

is absolutely a one-time thing. A one and only—"

"Mack, I'll call you in a few hours."

Al Kahtani is the only wanted man at large. He has a contract out on King who, he believes, is merely in hiding. The prosecuting attorney has a warrant out for Al Kahtani. There are currently 1,200 detectives, investigators, and FBI agents participating in the search, which starts in Sleepy Hollow and then branches out. They cover an enormous and massive area between Virginia and deeper and deeper north into new England.

"Hey, Mack."

"Hey, Fred. What you got?"

"I want you to take your guy, Robin, out of there. He should not be put at risk. My guys live the life every day—day by day. You got it?"

"This is what I've got to go on: they'll be in a shiny black new SUV or perhaps a large Lincoln sedan, perhaps both, but I doubt it. They are all dark-skinned, most of them bearded. They are Indian and Middle Eastern. They'll be in dark suits. They will either attempt to gain entry or attempt to accost Alia should she come out of or approach entry to her door."

"Okay, Mack. So that's it—thwart their plans and off 'em?"

"Fred. They should be followed the same day or night seen. Follow them to where they go—it is their hideout. And the leader of the pack is there. I need him gone, Fred. Take them all down at once. That leader is the big issue. The guy who most has to go."

"We can do that. We can do that. For you? Sure, man. For sure."

After the US marshal's office notifies Mack, he tells his daughter there is one lone man still looking for him and that the guy may come after her for ransom.

"Alia, listen to me. Robin will pick you up at 3:00 a.m. tonight...this coming morning. Meet him in the rear of your building. Behave as carefully and as secretive as you can. And Alia, this is the last of it. Promise. Be strong."

The Angels stake out Alia's condo in a dark gray van. Two others on bikes park a few spaces behind them. Three days and nights go by. Every twelve hours, Fred sends relief so no one gets too drowsy to handle the order. They question Fred about the operation, and he says to stay put. Follow the plan unless or until he tells them differently.

The fourth day comes with a surprise. The gloss black SUV pulls up and parks almost directly in front of Alia's entryway. There they wait all night long and into the next day. They remain throughout the following night. They are eating and using the facilities at Luigi's, a local favorite Italian joint. On the third day, they depart.

The Angels phone Fred and tell him they're tailing. Phone tracking is on. They are in South Boston, which used to be the Irish-Italian center of Boston culture.

They follow right to an abandoned tenement building.

"They are in the middle of the ghetto!"

They believe they find Kahtani's hideout. There is dim light coming from three rooms that they can see from their vantage point. They parked the bikes a couple blocks away so the noise wouldn't spook the profiles. The wanted men go right through the front door of the old building. Within moments, a few more broken windows shine dim light. Then almost all go out.

The Angels, under only the darkness of night, exit the van; all six guys carrying a knapsack and holstering a firearm. The only light is coming from the front side of the building, so they place the packs along the front; three to the left of the front door and three to the right. They go back to the van, and the two go to their bikes.

From two blocks away, they detonate the bombs. They waste no time returning to make sure all are dead. They climb over rubble to get in. The floors and ceilings above have all collapsed and lay at the ground floor. They quickly try to identify life. But there is none. They find the foreigners from the SUV dead. And they find Sanjay looking like he's been dead for a while. Further in, they find another sandman who is dressed all hipster-like; no suit for him. He lies face down, is gurgling and trying to speak and move. The Angels stand above him and on three blow six holes in the back of Al Kahtani's head.

An explosion in South Boston takes down an abandoned tenement building. No one on the prosecutor's team knows who carried out the hit, but Al Kahtani is identified among the dead. Evidence ties the few others found directly to him. There are no surveillance cameras around or in the defunct apartment house. The neighborhood was officially condemned years ago and on a list of areas around Boston to be redesigned modernly and rebuilt.

No suspects exist for the bombing. But a sloppy chore or two tie Sanjay Ganesh to the Hall and Cooper murders. Al Kahtani's DNA is found and matched virtually everywhere all over everything: Sleepy Hollow and in the Norfolk branch. It is assumed it was a contract killing put out by Al Kahtani's bosses, most of whom have been gathered together and are in the court system. Investigators into the bombing interview the project sponsors in custody. They get back a modest list of low-value suspects still running free.

"Marshall," Mack begins, "I would like to arrange contact with someone, communication and then possibly contact in person."

"Richard," the US marshal says, "it's funny you should mention that today."

"Why do you say that?"

"We have a request for communication and a tentative visit from someone for you! It just came through."

"Really? Who is it?"

"Brianna Croft."

"I do not know any Brianna Croft."

"Her previous name was Joan Dempsey. She's in WitPro too."

"Joan! Joan!"

"Yes. She requests communication and possible closer contact."

"Marshall, that is who I was about to request to contact just now! I shit you not."

In one of those synchronistic moments we experience in life, US marshalls receive requests from Mack and Joan to connect and perhaps visit each other—concurrently! Hell, half their jobs are done in this visitation case! "You've always been an easy guy to work with, Richard!"

"So what comes next?"

"She asks that we forward you her private phone number. So I'd say you initiate by calling her. We won't call her with your contact info unless you insist."

"No, no. Just give me her info, and I'll catch her up on things."

"Okay, you got it." The marshall hands an index card with only a phone number on it with a sharpie.

Mack sits deep on his living room recliner. The music plays soft, but he can hear every little nuance: every instrument and vocal part. Usually, he has to play it loud, but at this moment, it's different. His eyes are closed, and his visions of Joan fill every part of his mind that the music has not.

So cool, an adorably gorgeous and natural beauty.

She is classy but not snooty. And Mack fell in love with her starting the first day they met at the Sleepy Hollow lab. It was all he could do to stifle his attention away from her and to hold back the flirting he wanted to do to get her reading on him. He never had the chance to find out. She was most certainly polite, calm, and friendly toward him; but that could have been just part of her job. He thinks back. Did he ever do anything really stupid in front of her? He plans a call to her at around 7:00 p.m.

"Hey, you. It's Chuck."

"Hey, Chuck! What's up?"

"Al Kahtani and his hitmen won't be bothering you and your family any longer."

"Oh really?"

"Quite a thing: their hideout was bombed and an extra six caps went into Al Kahtani's skull, back of the head. Sends a signal."

"Any leads?"

"No. Nothing. No one at our end cares, truth be told. He was going to jail for life or get death, anyway."

"Thanks for the good news, Chuck. I'm very relieved."

"The trial will wind down in the next week. Maybe twelve days or so."

"Ugh, excellent. Big weight off the shoulders—hell—the HEAD!"

"Oh, I bet, and for us too."

"I really want to get Biomass Energy, Planet Fix going full bore."

"Don't forget, it has not stood stagnant

or dormant. The work continues every day according to your specifications. When you're back in full, I think you'll be quite surprised, impressed, pleased."

"That makes me very happy, man. Really happy."

"So there you go. Get on with your business, pal."

"Thanks for the great news, Chuck. We'll talk again soon."

"Okay, guy. Let's do."

"Bye just for now, man."

"Bye now, my friend."

Mack calls down to Alia, who is down in the rec room listening to music. It's quite loud, so Mack flicks the lights a few times to get her attention.

"Yeah, Dad?"

"Pack your bag, hon. It's time to go back home."

"I like it here, Dad!"

Mack laughs along with Alia, and she hollers. "Okay, Dad. I'll be ready in a few minutes and be right up."

It's just a twenty-five-minute fast drive from Mack's forest home to Alia's suburban town house. He walks her in. She keeps such a nice home.

"I just love this place of yours. And you keep it so nice and picked up."

"Dad, you say that every time you come here!"

"Oh, I'm repeating myself like two old ladies squawking over the clotheslines."

They both laugh. Alia is going to make coffee. "You want some, Dad?"

"Okay, yeah. I'd love a cup. Thank you."

He sits on her couch and thinks about Joan while waiting for his coffee. Alia delivers the coffee and comments, "You're quiet today, Dad."

"Well, Alia, I've got something on my mind."

"Like what?"

"You see, there's this woman—"

"Ohhhhh! *Someone* in your mind, you meant to say?" Alia cracks up laughing.

"All right, Alia, all right. Yes. I have someone in my mind."

"Where did you meet her? How?"

"Between me and you, she was the office manager in the lab I worked at in Sleeping Hollow."

"Oh my God, Dad! Did she get in trouble too?"

"Alia, I did not get in trouble with the law, and neither did she. But we have to hide because of the bad people we helped put away who did."

"So you both liked each other. Are ya gonna like get it together? Hook up?"

"That's what is on my mind, Alia. I have a date to call her on the phone tonight. This could be the start of something." He reaches.

"Were you friendly with each other when you worked together down there in New York?"

"We were both extrafriendly with each other. We flirted, okay? Yes. I think we both know that we like each other. Alia, I practically fell in love with her at first sight."

"Dad…Seriously? Please."

"So you don't believe in that. Okay, that's you. I keep the idea of it on the table. I am a believer that *all* things are possible. And besides, the vibes we shot back and forth at each other were unmistakable."

"Ugh, you and your vibes." Alia laughs in fun. She actually thinks her dad is cool.

"Alia, listen. I'll let know how things go tonight, and beyond."

"Really, Dad, I wish you could...I hope you really do fall in love again...with a good woman, who realizes what a great guy you are."

"Well, thank you, Alia. Thank you very much, sweetie."

"Okay. So tell me what she looks like! Does she wear makeup?"

Mack fixes a light supper and takes his time eating it. His mind is set on Joan or

Brianna; whatever they'll do. That will come with conversation. He can picture perfectly in his mind her looks: the red hair, the green eyes, the small nose, full lips, eyebrows nice and full-trimmed to perfection, dazzling complexion, buxom, slim waist, round rear end, and perfectly shaped legs. Her demeanor: classy yet amiable.

His thoughts make him a believer. He feels love. But he has to keep expectations low to squelch any disappointment that may will have come his way. How an oddity like this happens—is it pure synchronicity? Mack and Joan definitely share something, and he is almost ready to find out what it is. What if they're both thinking relationship? According to the US marshal, it can happen.

"Hello, Miss Brianna Croft?"

"Mister Richard Baldwin?" she asks with a chuckle. He joins in with laughter.

"So I guess you heard about our reaching out to each other within moments of each—" Mack begins.

"Yes. Yes, I did. What is that kind of a moment like that called?"

"*Synchronicity*. My younger self would merely call it fate or, worse, coincidence. Today, I declare it synchronicity. I've missed you so much, Joan."

"Mack, you've been in mind and thoughts ever since you left the labs. I was reprimanded just for asking about contact information."

"That was some crooked stuff going on. I found out late, but not too late, thank God."

"I am up on the *news* and current events: Mack, you are a genuine conquistador. Bringing down the unlawful, and then following that up with a global effort to convert fossil fuels to sustainable renewables? Wow."

"Yes. My kids told me I am considered some kind of man of goodness out there—some kind of hero." Mack laughs.

"Okay, so, I believe it is fine to use our names, Mack and Joan since we are on a secure VPN line," Joan says but with a question in her inflection.

"Yes, Joan, I agree and yes, the VPN is private, so I'll call you Joan unless you prefer Bri, and you can call me Mack. Good for you?"

"Perfect! Joan, please.

Mack, were all those feelings and vibes we shared for real? I will say mine were all genuine, and I fully admit that I felt myself falling in love with you."

"Joan, Joan. The feelings, the vibes were

real, and they all were sincere. I felt love too. And it never left my heart. I loved you at our greeting at reception."

"Mack," Joan begins, "I want to see you. I really do. What do you think of that?"

"Nothing could be any lovelier is what I say to that, Joan. Please come. Come to my place, please, Joan. It is quiet. It is beautiful. It is pure nature and peaceful. It would be a great change for you—soothing."

"Mack, that is exactly what I hoped you'd say and would like to do. Thank you."

"Well, let's both call our respective Marshalls and let them know our plans. I say we do it tomorrow morning!" Mack let's out a subtle snicker. He sounds like a junior high boy. Joan giggles.

"Capital idea, Mack. After we do that,

let's talk—early afternoon—and share what we took away from our Marshalls."

"Okay, Joan, you make your call, and I'll make mine. Let's plan on talking at, say, 1:00 p.m. Okay with you?"

"Superb, Mack. Talk tomorrow. Have a good night."

"Thanks. You too."

All of the sponsors, stakeholders, initiators, and the knowing pawns are on their way to prison. There is time to do and millions in fines to pay. Undermining the oil business and governments is one thing. But causing the damage by way of the fault created, and the continuation of that, remains another count against them all. Cracking the nadir has split the earth.

No one could've guessed that the richest oil nations would do such a thing: they certainly do not need the reserves. But Mack knows why. The people who controlled Advanced Energy used the resources harvested and saved the rest. Their cost per barrel remained at $12, thus, undermining OPEC and other oil-rich nations. All their business was off the books in any official capacity, but well in hand privately.

Most of the higher-ups were in or very near billionaire status just before the bust. Cleaning up the mess at the ocean floor is expensive, and much of that expense is picked up by the fines levied against those who were in power behind Advanced Energy. They will also pay for the damage to shoreline properties and islands that were not completely decimated. Closing the line in the nadir and plugging up the Mid-Atlantic coasts are also an extra supplementary expense.

Two of the men were found hanging from a top tier crossbar. They used sheets. The rest were placed in maximum security and on twenty-four-hour watch. These people have nothing. A bed with a plastic mattress, a toilet and small sink all bolted to the floor. And every night, they hear the shuffle of a loved one's feet. But no, it's just the guards'.

Some nights, men cry out drearily and weepy, while the others yell out for them to shut up. They are given toothbrushes and paste that they have to return as soon as they are done. They take showers separate from the other prison population. They receive death threats: no one minds a crook, but a crook in big business and especially the government, ripping lower-level society off is out of bounds.

They realize they are much safer being

put away alone in an 8' × 12' cell and keep separate from the general prison population. Many will die there. The other younger ones *may* get out in time to wander around the new world feeding pigeons or playing checkers on a park bench before they too will succumb to age and ailments. Some families break away, never to be seen or heard from again. A few remain solid within their clan and visit whenever they possibly can: true blue.

The Department of Justice, the AG, FBI, DOD, and several local and state law enforcement officials continue their duties to make sure the bad guys are caught, and any other who are implicit associates and conspirators are brought in for questioning. Some show up with lawyers and others do not, which peculiarly point to those conscience-stricken, and those innocent, or at least who have nothing to hide.

"Mack, it's Chuck," Chuck begins. "We also have John conferenced in."

"Well, I'll tap the keg!" Mack laughs along with his two besties.

"Chuck will start," John says. "Then I'll come in."

"Mack," Chuck begins, "the trials are over. We've got them all. Now, that does not mean you come out of WitPro. There is absolutely no way to know if there remain any loyalists, followers or vengeful, and the like, you see."

"I fully understand. But hey, man, that's great *news*!"

"Yeah, we got those !

"Thanks to you, Mr. Mack."

"I had to, Chuck. When I began to understand the true objective and all else, I knew I had to blow the whistle no matter who was involved or how high-up they were. And I thank you for moving on it based on those reports—crazy as they must've read to you!"

"It took a few reads, but I got, and got it good. The hardest part was doing it all under the secretary of state. Once I had it coordinated, formulated, and up to standard, and mass arrests were taking place, bringing the secretary in was just natural progression. Due to the gravity of the crimes, the classification was easily understood."

"Weight...gone," Mack says.

"Mack, I don't know where to begin," John says. "It's all too good."

"Well, damn it, man. Tell it!" Mack replies, laughing.

"Mack, the crops are thriving across the

nation. The revolution is rolling on just like you said they would. The tobacco trade is on, the mills are fabricating garments, the energy processing centers are at peak capacity, automobile companies are fully cooperating and converting vehicles and building new ones to run on clean energy."

"Fantastic! I've never been so happy. I've never felt so good about work I've done."

"There's more, buddy."

"Blow my mind, John. Go ahead!"

"Okay, significant progress and in areas popping up everywhere, biomass energy is spreading across Western Europe already."

"Like where, for example?"

"Like in the Netherlands, Germany, Belgium, Austria, Switzerland, France, Spain, and Portugal."

"Wow, that's great!"

"And Mack," John says. "The East is right on the West's tails. They are in process and will be up and running within eighteen months. You know how those Japs are! Heh, heh."

"How many jobs added, John?"

"We have created, in all, over a million and a half jobs, most of which are permanent."

"Excellent! Huh, John? Wow!"

"History in the making, my genius friend."

"Okay, John, time for a little dinner. Take care till next time, huh."

"Absolutely, you do too."

Mack daydreams of his upcoming time with Joan. He sees them sleeping later than usual. He plans his morning coffee and hikes, then he'll treat her to brunch. They'll go out whenever the spirit moves. He'd like most to relax and talk with her. He really wishes to speak with her about them. Them as a couple. Sure it seems soon, but given their past together, which counts as courtship if you ask him, and she seems open!

The long talks, the long looks, the shared lunches, the eye contact and the eyes, those smiling eyes. Her fluid voice, smooth as syrup, and most of all her manners. There are some signs you cannot ignore, and there are feelings that you cannot bury. Speaking with her brought it all back, not that it had wandered far, but put her right back in his forefront. He longs to hold her.

"Hey, Robin!"

"Mack! What's up?"

"I want to ask a favor."

"Sure, buddy, what can I do for ya?"

"Well, I have to pick up a friend at the Portland Jet Port. It's kind of a special rekindling. I'd like you to drive me down there in my long black Mercedes, then return us here. On the way back, I'd like to sit with her in the back. I'll sit with you on the way down, of course."

"Sure, man, I can do that—no problem."

"I'll drop $100 on ya for the time and trouble."

"Come on, Mack, Jesus. Do I get to wear the cool dark-blue suit and little hat?"

Mack walks home with Joan all over his mind. He's been so lonesome for so long. He hopes his home isn't too dusty. He's got to clean and shop for groceries, although they agreed they would do that together. A fleeting thought crosses his mind. Is she a natural redhead? He can't help it.

She'll be here in a few days, so he proceeds to clean the house now. The thought of her—the vision—keeps him going nonstop until he is done with placement, scrubbing, dusting, and polishing. He vacuums the following day. He is satisfied, but he wants some air cleaner, so he goes to the big box store. He buys some four spray cans and several plug-in style. He prefers the organic Blue Magic.

There is a central vac hidden away in the daylight basement, and there are valves for the vacuum in house. The long hose and brush cleaner and wand stays stored in one of the hall closets upstairs. He checks that all the beds are made and clean as he roams the house with his magic wand and roller brush.

He sits in his living room recliner when he finishes and, in his mind, thinks through every room to convince himself that no place was forgotten. Ah, he goes to his office. There is work to be done. Straightening out the few piles of paper and putting things where they belong is it, and he is done. He goes back to the living room, reclines. And while thinking of Joan, falls easily into a deep sleep. He dreams of her.

He sits in his fishbowl in Sleepy Hollow. He sees her walking his way. She blows him a kiss as she turns to her right and gives him the most sensual expression he's ever seen. And as this plays repeatedly, his level of emotion rises. And every time she knocks on the door to come in, he gets the butterflies. He motions her in with a smile, and their eyes never leave each other's. Her smile is gleaming, and her eyes are wide.

As she addresses him *Mr. King*, he asks her to please call him Mack when they are away from the group. She repeats his name, "Mack," then "King," then, finally, softly, slowly, "Mack King, Mack King." And she smiles so sweetly, looking him right in the eyes.

"Please call me Joan."

She had him from that first meeting, and he feels like there is reciprocity there. They flirt in all flavors of ways, day in and day out, no one the better to know or notice. The that come involuntarily whenever they are close, in chairs, standing, in the elevator, are a tangible sense of exactly what is going on between them.

He wonders if she feels it too. But he's always been a great assessor of character and interpreter of vibes. Time mellows the liquidity of mood and tender of feelings as it does a barrel of bourbon. Admittedly, he did indeed falls for her the moment they met in the reception area.

Mack answers the door. It's Robin. They decided on casual wear. It's an hour to the Jet Port, so Mack offers Robin a cocktail. They both decide on Mack's favorite, bourbon. "You want it like mine?"

"Oh yeah, that'll be fine."

"I do a double shot, a cube, twist of lime, and a splash of ginger ale."

"Sounds great! I've never had one quite like this before."

"Well, cheers, my brother!"

"Cheers, Mack!"

They sip and relax before it's time to leave. Mack puts on an old favorite Donald Fagan album on low. "Are you sure you don't want me to do the drive south, Robin?"

"Positive! I want to do the whole thing."

"Just keep your eyes on the road once she's in the back. I know it's gonna be difficult, but fight it man, fight it!"

Both men are laughing loud. They've already talked about dinner all together and other things. Mack wants to include Robin in some of the experiences. Granted, most of her time there will be spent solely with Mack.

"Okay, Robin. Drop me at the baggage door's curb and circle around until you see us out here with her stuff. Okay?"

"Got it, boss." Robin laughs.

"Not that I believe you could ever it up!" Now Mack is laughing.

"All right, here I go. You get in there and gather up your babe."

"Okay. We'll be out soon."

Mack stations himself near the chute of the baggage carousel and glances around when he sees people heading his way. Out of courtesy, he stands back a little. He sees her from a distance. The natural and earth tones she is wearing go beautifully on her skin, all ivory and golden undertones. Her legs look so fine, outstanding with gold low heels.

He has a foundational smile plastered on his face as he sees her coming. She sees him and smiles that smile and habitually pushes her short hair behind her ears. She can't stop smiling, either. She reaches him and opens her arms, and they embrace in a long gentle hug.

"So good to see you, Mack."

"Joan, I've dreamt of this moment."

They watch for her bags, and as she says

there's one, he grabs it out of the line. She has three suitcases and her carry-on. She carries one, and he two.

"Come outside. The car will be coming around in a moment."

"The car?"

"You didn't park in the lot?"

"No, my one and only neighbor, Robin, insisted on having us sit together in the back on the way back north. He knows how special this occasion is for us. He's a heck of a good guy. You'll like him."

"That's so nice," Joan says in that irresistible tone of voice.

Mack sees his car approaching. "Okay, Joan, here we go."

He opens the back door and has her slide in. He takes care of her luggage, putting it in the spacious trunk. He gets in the back and right away introduces Joan to Robin.

"Too late, Mack," Robin says. "I've already introduced myself!"

"Well, we're all good then. Home please, Mr. Robin!" The two men laugh, and Joan lets out a soft chuckle.

"How far do you live from the Jet Port, Mack?"

"Well, about fifty minutes to my property, then another twenty or thirty minutes to the house."

Mack and Joan talk about his neighborhood, his property and home. He'll have Robin drive the mile down to his place, then Mack will drive back to his place.

"This property is fabulous. I can't wait to see it in full daylight!"

"It is quite nice, Joan. I hope you'll be comfortable here."

"I'm sure I will be. You can give me the grand tour inside when we get there." She chuckles.

Mack parks the car in the garage next to the Rover but suggests they walk out and around to enter through the front door.

"I'm following you, sweet man."

The front porch is covered and ran across the middle third of the house's length. Joan admires the wrought-iron bistro table and chairs.

"Okay, we're in! Let me get the bags in here first."

He brings them in and sets them down, lined up at the far end of the foyer. Joan steps in and, with an audible gasp, practically chokes on her words. "Oh, Mack. This is magnificent!"

"I am quite pleased and satisfied with it."

"It looks like it's been decorated by a professional. No offense."

"It was." He smiles broadly. "Under only my instructions. Most everything was done for me before I moved in, but according to my specifications. As you will see, I quite like primitive colonial, folklore, and shaker-style design."

"I am realizing it already."

"Does it appeal to you, Joan? I like the simply complex nature of the fundamental sturdy. I like folk art too as you'll notice."

"Oh I love it, Mack! Oh my God, is that a real Mission Oak chair?"

"I want to put your bags away before we tour and then relax."

"Yes?"

"Well, Joan…" Mack stammers, "um…would you prefer private quarters?"

"Oh, Mack, you are so sweet." She looks directly into his eyes and replies, "Mack, I want to stay with you. Is that all right?"

"Joan, that would be my preference. I want to lie and rest with you—nice and close—skin to skin." And he smiles, looking straight into her eyes now.

"Well then, have a seat here in the living room while I carry your bags downstairs to the master bedroom."

"Nonsense! I am helping carry my own bags, Mr. Mack!" They both laugh as they pick up the luggage. Mack leads the way. Joan takes it all in as they cross the immense dining area and through the large kitchen. They round the corner on the laundry room, and she follows him down the stairs.

"Oh, Mack, there's another entire home down here!" They walk through a small living area and enter a tremendously large rec room. There is a built-in bookcase along on entire wall. There is another media center there and opposite a sitting area.

"This is a spare room." Mack points to a bedroom they pass by.

"Here we are." They organize her stuff in the large walk-in closet. She sets up her toiletries in the connected bath. He stands watching, smiling. She turns quickly around and catches him looking at her so lovingly.

"Aww, Mack. Come here, you!" And they come together in a hug everlasting, caressing each other their backs. They look at each other enchanted and kiss. The kiss they need and want. The kiss they've longed for. The kiss that lasts forever.

"I suggest we go upstairs and enjoy an adult beverage, my dear."

"Capital idea, Mr. Mack."

"Are you comfortable, I mean in the clothes you traveled in?"

"Yes, I'm fine for now. Let's go."

On the way up, he points out different things she might be interested in. He takes her through the entire floor; two more bedrooms, another one made into an office and another full bath. Besides the shaker style and primitive colonial treatments, she notices the floors and the countertop.

"Well, the floors in the kitchen and baths are Grecian tile, the rest are hardwood, except the bedrooms and closets, which are opal-colored Berber carpet. The countertop is classic butcher block," he answers her questions.

"I adore the wrought-iron hardware and the punched tin switch plates. Sockets and lampshades are so comforting to see. This whole place whispers 'Welcome.'"

He leads her to the divan and asks what she'll have. He returns with the drinks. "Cheers, dear Joan."

"To you, Mr. Mack."

They sit together in silence a moment or two: they both have questions for each other. He decides to breach the silence with something light. "So how is your place down in Fort Lauderdale?"

"It's a high-rise, and I'm on the eighth floor. It's fairly spacious—all I need, anyway. And it's right across the street from the beach."

"Did you design it?"

"No. But I do like it all right. I was just delivered to it. I imagine we went through the same or similar book of rules and all."

"I suppose we did. I was all wound up in the Biomass, criminal activity, and trial court."

"See, I was kept shielded from all of that. I didn't even ask for WitPro."

"Joan, I initiated that. I also protected Mofty."

"Virtually everyone, everybody was suspect, and most knew nothing about what was going on. Can you tell me—abridged if you prefer—what that was all about?"

"Joan, I'll share the short story, but powerful one, because I love you."

"Mack, I love you too. But I feel like I have to know."

"That is incredible! All that devastation at the hands of Kahtani."

"Yes. As soon as I figured it all out, I wrote the 'Whistler Report' and following that, the testimony that nailed Kahtani for horizontally drilling under the United States' east coast. I was into the Biomass and Planet Fix at the same time too."

"Many of those under the sponsors and stakeholders were apprehended. Some committed suicide before the authorities could get to them. It's a shame because they could have all made a deal for their testimony. Two of the sponsors hung themselves in jail."

"So we were involved in a global crisis."

"Yes, we were. Joan, listen. In the end, Kahtani and Ganesh were in hiding and hunting down the project managers like me. They somehow got close to my daughter, so I hired some friends of mine, the Hell's Angels, to take them out. They did, and the DNA recovered tied everything together: Ganesh murdering Hall and Cooper, and Kahtani killing Ganesh. And Kahtani's prints and DNA were everywhere in Sleepy Hollow, Norfolk and the apparatus used to commit the crimes."

"Goodness gracious. Damn!"

"So no worries anymore, but we must all remain in WitPro just for safe measure."

"I have no problem with that!"

"Joan, I have to tell you something because I think you deserve to know."

"Okay."

"I was a millionaire before joining the

project. I've worked very hard over the years in information sciences. I was good and in demand, and all of a sudden, I found myself bringing home $1,500 a day. It all added up pretty quickly.

"But the project paid me a salary of $11 million per project phase, plus bonuses and incentives. I had no idea it was lowdown till midway through." He takes her hand in his and, looking down, says, "Joan my net worth today is $26 million and growing. I keep a minimal balance of $100,000 in my local credit union. I live off dividends."

"Mack, is the money clean?"

"Yes, Joan, it is. If not for me, the earth would be split in two, and the Atlantic Ocean would be gone, among other crisis. But listen to this:

have you paid attention to the movement to Biomass Energy and the Planet Fix projects?"

"Yes, somewhat. I'm not an expert, but I get what it's all about. I would like to hug the person behind the change the people of this country have cried and marched for decades."

Mack looks up. He gently holds her hand and holds her chin up with the other and looks her in the eyes. He squeezes her hand. He cries.

"What, baby?" Joan is confused. "Please tell me. You'll feel better."

"Joan, I am that man. I wrote and designed the Biomass Energy and Planet Fix projects."

"Oh, Mack! Mack! It's you! You are the hero. The folk hero remaining anonymous. Everyone on earth wants to know you, of you. How noble, my baby. Don't cry. Come here."

She pulls him in for a snug, tight hug. "Everything's okay," she says.

"Ask of me anything you want to, Joan. I want it all open and honest between us—with me and you—from the very start."

"So this activists' movement is on its way globally? And our country is practically done leading the way? Renewables, new crops to keep the planet and the people healthier? Tobacco imported, cannabis legal, so many great, long in coming and more, Here, today?"

"Yes, sweetheart."

"Because of you! Mack! You did it!"

"Yes. This is true."

"May I ask you something?"

"Of course."

"Well, given your contribution and participation—being the architect of world change—what is your salary from Biomass and Fix?"

"I refused any money. I insisted against it. But they direct deposit into my Fidelity policy $5 million once a year."

She gently pulls him into her, his head rested on a breast, arm around her waist. Her arm around his back. They sit slouched on the couch for twenty-five minutes. He seems a little restless, so she tells him to sit tight. She's going to fix a couple new drinks.

"How much of this property do you own?"

"I own the entire 875-acre lot. The clearing around the crowned home is about ten acres. Besides the small plot I gave to Robin, the land is meadow in the center and forests surrounding. I'll take you for a walk tomorrow through the meadows—they are beautiful, and wild berries grow everywhere."

"Well, if we, er…you ever decide to get your hands in the earth you've got plenty of room to do it!" Joan laughs, then asks Mack, "Are you all right, honey?"

"Yes, babe. I just got a little emotional. I'm sitting with the woman, the only woman I love, whom I ever want to love, the one who defines it."

"I feel the same about you, Mack."

"When I mixed money into the equation, I just tightened up. I'm sorry. I'm fine. Really, I am."

"Let's sit and sip for a few."

"Okay."

Robin knocks at the front door. No answer. He knocks more. He rings the doorbell. He goes to the back daylight basement door and bangs as hard as he can. There is a ship's bell mounted there, so he yanks on the woven tassel. It's loud. He knocks again.

Finally, Mack comes to the door. Robin can tell that he just crawled out of bed. The door opens hard. They hardly ever use it.

"Robin, hey, what's up?"

"I just wanted to let you know that there are two suspicious black cars parked at the end of your lane."

"Get a look at them?"

"No, man, I didn't want to seem suspicious or cause any trouble."

"You did the right thing, Robin. Thanks. I'll check it out right now."

Mack hears Joan calling. He goes back to the bedroom, and before he can say anything, she whispers to him, licking her lips, "Last night was wonderful. Mmm."

Mack bends over her side and gives her a hug and a kiss and says, "Because of you, sweetness."

"Who was at the door?"

"Robin. I have to go check something out. Just have to make a phone call for now. Relax. I'll be right back." Mack goes upstairs to his office. He picks up his phone and punches in the number. It's ringing. *Shit, man. Pick up.*

"United States Marshals," the man finally answers.

"This is Richard C. Baldwin with an urgent call for my agent, please."

"Please hold."

"Richard! Everything okay with Brianna?"

"Couldn't be better, thanks."

"So what's up?"

"There are two black shiny cars parked at the end of my lane. They've been there quite a while. And I'm getting a little nervous. Especially with Joan here, I mean Brianna. Can you handle it, please? Let me know what you find?"

"Course, man! I'll shoot right over and look things over."

"Thanks, man. You're the best."

"I'll call ya."

"All right. Bye."

"Yup."

"Okay, Sully!"

"Yeah, boss."

"You're dressed down? I need you to case for me. Put on your cap. Wear it backwards."

"Take the wrangler and head down to Ridley Lane. There are a couple suspicious cars parked there. They are waiting for something. Act lost. Just get them talking and take a reading. I'll be at the top of the hill leading to the lane. Come back to me there and debrief."

"You got it."

Sully swerves and rambles down the hill toward Ridley. He stops then goes. He does that twice then drives slowly up to the two black cars. He eyeballs the men in the driver's seats. Long black hair, trimmed beards, dark skin. The cars are parked in a one Adam 69, and so Sully chugs up to the car with the driver on his side.

"Scuse me, hoss. I might be a little bit lost here."

The Arabian just stares at him.

"So where am I here? Do you know the name of this road here?"

The dark man swings his door open and jumps out. He grabs Sully by the neck and holds a handgun to his head. Sully is on his knees thinking of what he can do to get out of this.

The US marshal at the top of the hill walks down, careful not to be seen. He rounds the corner at the bottom of the hill. He sees Sully under the gun. At that moment, the other suited man gets out of his car and reaches for his weapon.

Four crackling explosions ring from the woods.

The man falls right on top of Sully. The top of his head rolls away.

A voice comes from the woods just a couple hundred feet up the lane. "Drop your weapon you sack-a-shit, or you're next. Hear me? Dead man! Dead man! Okay YOU are a dead man in three, two, one!"

"Okay, okay, okay." And the weapon drops to the ground.

"Now kick it away, asshole! I said *do it now*!"

Mack's US marshal walks up to the lane.

"US Marshal Tierney, please identify yourself. Robin, Robin come down here and assist me, please."

Robin walks toward the live one and spits on the ground.

"Robin, I want you to keep your weapon

point blank at this ragtop's head. If he moves, shoot him. You got that?"

"Yes, sir."

"Okay, sandman, open that head of yours up and tell me what is going on here, or my friend Robin will open it for you."

"We were hired by a Saudi named Omar El Mofty. He said the man who lives on this road could do him grave harm. He hired us to just kill the man, leave him, and get back to Arabia ASAP."

"Well, it looks like the man on this road already did one of you in. Think I should turn him loose on you too?"

"No. Please. Obviously there has been some mistake. Eh? Yes?"

"Let me borrow that .357 hole-maker, Robin."

Three thundering shots decimates the Arabian head.

"Okay, Robin, we'll get your man in his trunk and then get my man into the other trunk. We're going to the back side of Sabattus Lake. Open all the windows, put a weight on the accelerator, let 'em go and let 'em sink. We do it together. Got that?"

Tierney radios into the bureau. Robin is delivered to his home.

"Robin. Not one word of this to Mack. Do you understand?"

"Yes, sir."

"I mean it. Not a word. Think of something clever."

The marshal is taken back to his vehicle. He drives to the office.

Number one: a contract on one Omar El Mofty. He's walking dead.

Number two: a comfort call to Mack.

"Just a couple hunters looking for 'No Hunting' warning signs."

Mack and Joan decide right away to apply for a domestic partnership; $35 bucks, and you're hitched! Plus, it can be done privately. She keeps the condo in Florida for a winter getaway for Mack and herself. She ships only belongings she cannot do without the cold, snow and ice up in Maine.

Mack lies in bed and every night thanks Jesus for reassuring him that this truth Joan would join him forever.Thanks and praise for blessings.

And good Karma comes around every night.

The End